God's Signature Tune

God's Signature Tune

Jack U. Nwolisa

Newburgh Press,
Newburgh, Indiana
2017

God's Signature Tune

Newburgh Press
Newburgh, Indiana
2017

Dedication

This book, based on my dissertation, was possible because of revealed knowledge from God and as such is being dedicated first to God and then to my family.

To my wife Christy for constantly supplying the comfort and peace needed in the family which enabled me to concentrate on the assignment.

To my children, Arinze, Nkoli, Chika and Ikem, whose support and encouragement made it easier for me to complete this work and for me to share it with the world.

To my sister Ifeoma, whose prayers and knowledge of God's love for her brother played a great role in helping me begin the journey towards fulfilling my calling.

Nothing matters much in life than the will to succeed in becoming what God has created you to be.

For every question and for every problem, there is a
scripturally promised answer and scripturally promised solution.
Remembering the 'What', 'How' and 'Why' of the true Bible
which I have called God's signature tune will take you there.

Acknowledgement

To Newburgh Theological Seminary (NTS) Staff and specially Dr. Glenn Mollette for making it possible for this dissertation to be printed and published as a book to God's glory and honor. To my sponsor, Dr. Femi Falana of Redeem Bible College and Seminary Texas USA, who showed me where to put my effort for this next level in my pursuit for more. I say, I am grateful and thankful and that your introducing me to this prestigious institution, Newburgh Theological Seminary for this TH. D program is highly appreciated and will always be remembered. My dissertation could not have been possible without the recommended books which did stretch me beyond my own imagination. Those books are great and the definitions and illustrations from C.S. Lewis on His Mere Christianity along with A.W. Tozer in his book 'The Pursuit of God' added more to my knowledge and understanding of the Bible. Christian theology was a master piece, so also Robert Louis Wilkens book on the Spirit of Early Christian Thought. I can only say big thank you to Newburgh Theological Seminary staff and the grading crew. Dr. John Sloan, my adviser, the Registrar Sandy East will always be remembered for their concerns to make sure that I had all I may need to go through the program. I will always show my appreciation to Newburgh Theological Seminary because of the increase in knowledge from my reading and studying most of the books I went through for my course work. They are good, very informative books and I will always recommend anyone of kind looking for such. The no travel seminars were awesome and I thank the intellectuals that contributed to Newburgh Theological Seminary dignity and integrity. Well done Newburgh Theological Seminary, more grease to your elbows. I do hope that my future academic pursuit will bear the mark of Newburgh Theological Seminary.

Introduction

God wants us to know and always remember that there is a biblically promised solution to every encounter in one's life. From Genesis to Revelation, God has demonstrated his capability, His availability and His Willingness to provide and protect us, spiritually, physically and emotionally. Understanding the 'What, How and Why' of the true Bible which I have called, God's signature tune will take you to locating these scriptural promised answers and solutions to every question asked and every problem of life. From the inception of our covenant relationship, God did establish this promise. Psalm 145:13b NLT said it also, "the Lord always keeps His promises, He is gracious in all He does". The purpose of this dissertation is to add to and increase the amount of reliable scriptural knowledge of God's intentions to His creation. The Bible is all about God. It contains the words of God and it's a record of events written down by God's inspired people. From Genesis to Revelation, it's all about What God said and What He did, How He said it and How He did it, and finally Why He said it and Why He did it. God spoke the universe into existence with everything in perfect order. He said let us (Father, Son and Holy Spirit) make man in our own image and after our likeness, Genesis 1 & 2. But what happened after this marvelous and miraculous creation of the universe, is what is being asked? Who is responsible and under whose jurisdiction is it going to be fixed? What are the consequences of this collapse if left unattended? We ask the questions and God Has the answers. Whatever God has said and done is always followed by How it is said, and Why it is said and done. Remember that God always speaks His wish into existence. As God told Elijah to go there in 1st Kings 17:4, so also He is telling us today that for every problem or question, there is a How to do it out there. What God said and did was good originally, but suddenly went bad. Why and How did this happen? Only God who created the universe and also created the man that messed up His purpose and plans, knew what happened, How it happened and why it happened. He only has the answers to those questions. What did God say and did to amend the broken relationship, how and why he did, what He said. There are about three ways that come to mind, regarding God's process which the Trinity used to bring about the reconciliation, restoration and restructuring.

(1) One may go through it by way of covenants and dispensation

(2) One may go through the Old Testament and New Testament series.

(3) Divide the Bible into four parts that is, Old testament into part 1 and 2 and New Testament into part 3 and 4.

I will go through the 3rd route. First, the Old Testament divided into 2 parts; events before Moses (before Mount Sinai) and after Moses (events after Mount Sinai). That is before the law and after the law was given. Part 3 and 4. Part 3 deals with before Jesus went to the cross. Part 4 deals with after Jesus had gone to the cross. My choosing this route was based on 2nd Timothy 2:15(Amp). Here the book of Timothy is telling believers How to study the bible and I quote, "Study and be eager and do your utmost to present yourself to God approved (tested by trial) a workman who has no cause to be ashamed, correctly analyzing and accurately dividing (rightly handling and skillfully teaching) the Word of truth". So, answers and solutions must be derived from God's revealed truth. You should study the bible to know your responsibilities and what belongs to you. Know what God has provided, promised, confirmed and established. Know what are examples, promises, wishes, contrasts and comparisons in the bible. Remember that authority goes with responsibility. We should realize in the first place that un-informed people must know that there is a God to be believed, a God to be trusted, who had been disappointed by His creation. The God who spoke the universe into existence and up-holding all things by the Word of His power, as said in Hebrews 1:3. Remember, God's power is voice activated. Many people have written about the bible, about God's relationship with His creation, yet what God said and did, how he said it and did it and why He said it and did it, has been in short supply. The purpose and significance, of this What, How and Why of God is what the dissertation has come to address. To let you know what promises that are of God and the ones that are of man. How to locate, distinguish and apply them as a game changer in your life. You will observe also that it has been the unfolding of the truth concerning redemption that are being narrated from Genesis to Revelation.

Table of Contents

PART ONE

Adam: Before the Law and Before Moses

Chapter 1
The Book of Genesis

The book of Genesis is divided into two main sections. The first 11 chapters deals with the history of human race and the last 39 chapters with the family of Abram. As is written in the Bible, God created the universe by speaking it into existence. After seeing that all of His creation was good, Genesis 1:10-18, and all created after its kind, He turned to create man along with the Trinity Genesis 1:26. In Genesis 1:28, "God blessed them and said unto them, Be fruitful and multiply and replenish the earth, and subdue it and have dominion over the fish of the sea, and over the fowl of the air, and over every living thing that moveth upon the earth". Adam was placed in a comfortable part of this universe, the Garden of Eden with everything to make life pleasurable. God's purpose was for relationship, intimacy and fellowship. Thanking Him, praising Him and worshipping Him was their concern and God's concern. Mirroring God's glory and reflecting it back to Him was man's measure for gratitude. The family in the Garden was the type of family in anticipation for the rest of mankind through Adam and Eve. There were no enemies to bind and loose, no demons to cast out, no mother in laws or outlaws to encounter, and no enemies to contend with. Adam was aware of what God said and did, How He said it and did it and why He said it. When Adam's helper arrived, Adam was happy and named her Eve as he has named all other animals. They were operating in the sixth sense, faith. All of what the garden can produce and ever will produce were for Adam and Eve and for their children yet to arrive. God told Adam that of every tree of the garden thou mayst freely eat, Genesis 2:16. But of the tree of the knowledge of good and evil, thou shall not eat of it, for in the day that thou eatest thereof thou shalt surely die. This was clear to Adam, Genesis 2:17. The only labor required of Adam was thanking God, praising Him and worshiping Him, that was all. No tares or weeds to uproot in the Garden of Eden as there were no known enemies around.

Chapter 2
Adam's Disobedience

Suddenly what God said was good has now gone terribly bad. What has happened? The problem is not simple and the answer is not going to be easy either. Adam and the wife have messed up the covenant Adam had with God. The relationship has broken, the intimacy gone and the fellowship has shifted away. I am sure Adam didn't know the consequences of what he has done nor able to estimate the damage he has done to mankind. Adam could have prevented Satan's deceit when Eve decided to be the spokesperson. She was not there when God and Adam went into covenant. Adam and Eve now knew that they were naked and needed something to cover their nakedness. Satan perverted the What of God and the How of God and the Why of God, to deceive Eve. Has God said that? And How can you just die by touching that tree? Touch it and see if you will die? Eve touched it and didn't die, even though she didn't know what was death, and so since the first proof is a lie then the second may also be a lie. So, Eve, who didn't die after touching the tree, did eat and gave to her husband Adam and he also ate and at that instance their eyes were open. Walking together in the cool of the day ended and the created problem must be fixed by God. So many writers have noted, that throughout history it has been the inaction of those who should have acted, in this case Adam, and the indifference of those who should have known better, in this case Adam, and the silence of the voice of justice when it mattered most that has made it possible for evil to triumph, again, Adam was responsible.

How was Eve deceived? Adam could have used the What, Why and How of God to avoid the disaster but instead kept silent, secret and allowed Satan to pervert God's What, Why, How, to deceive Eve through the lust of the flesh, the lust of the eye and the pride of life. God touched us first at creation and now a second touch of redemption is needed. Everything bad originated from here, sin, disobedience, fear, doubt, unbelief excuses, unforgiveness all have their root here. This is normally referred to as first mentioned theory. Their eyes were opened to behold all things considering their own sinfulness, because of their spiritual eyes been closed and their physical eyes open. This will be a long process and how long it will take comes under God's jurisdiction, His Sovereignty. God wants us to use this how and why to sort out the problems and questions of the world since "we are living in a part of the universe occupied by rebel" (Lewis 1980, 45). "Christian view that this is a good world that has gone wrong, but still retains the memory of what it ought to have been. The other is the view of Dualism with the belief that there are two equal and independent powers at the back of everything, one of them good and the other bad, and that this universe is the battlefield in which they fight out an endless war" (Lewis 1980, 42). It looks as if we humans are cut in between, like the sailors in Jonah who were cut in between God and Jonah. Who knows? What happened to Adam happened to some other people in the Bible. This single act of rebellion, unknown and unrealized by Adam and Eve did set in motion unprecedented reactions, shifts, negative imaginations, hence disorganizing the settled order of God's plan towards mankind. This scenario has continued to repeat itself in human history at times called the reoccurring decimal in science or in mathematics. Think of Elijah in the book of Kings. Elijah heard what God said and was aware of How He said it and why He said it and yet went home with excuses and caused the misfortune of other people, 1st Kings 19:15-17. Many people who could have lived were killed because of Elijah's neglect and this issue lingered for many years until Hazael became king of Syria and Jehu king of Israel.

Chapter 3

God's Relationship with Adam

During the period before God approached Noah, a lot have happened, a lot of evil was going on, prompting God to initiate a process of solution to bring mankind back to Himself. Adam had two sons, Cain and Abel. Cain later killed his brother Abel out of pride and jealousy. God never imputed Cain's sin into his record. Mankind was using Cain's murder as an excuse or as a reference point to cover all sorts of evil. God dealt with Cain so mildly that his sin was over looked in many circles. The wickedness of man was so much that God had to do something fast to redeem mankind, Genesis 6:5-6. The dispensation of conscience was based on Adam's limited experience with good and evil.

God approached Noah to build an ark and prepare for God's cleansing. The known world mocked and ridiculed Noah but Noah stood His ground, saying that he clearly heard from God. God gave him all the specifications, length, width, depth, the wood to use and so on. For one hundred and twenty years Noah labored in building the ark. Here again, God told Noah what to do, how to do it and why he will do it that way. Noah received the what, the How and why of God and obeyed it to completion. The problem that has persisted has been our unwillingness to believe what we even know is the truth and that truth is from God. Noah could have waved it off as not coming from God. He was dancing the tune of God and God was directing his path. Noah knew it was the voice of God, the signature tune of God and so he went to work brushing aside all distractions, ridicules, mockery and shame brought to him. He was called all sorts of names, but Noah insisted to run with the tune he has heard from God. The sheep is sensitive to the voice of the shepherd.

God made a covenant with Noah, Genesis 6:18. Noah finished the building, loaded the ark accordingly and there comes the rain and the flooding that swallowed the known whole world leaving Noah and all that the ark was carrying, peaceful and alive. Gods instruction to Noah select a pair of all created species was so that God need not go back and start creation afresh. God knows the end from the beginning and as such remembered Noah and caused the ark to land, resting on the mountains of Ararat. Noah obeyed God and showed appreciation, by building an altar and offering a burnt sacrifice to God for His concerns and love for Him and his family with the rest of the creatures, animals, everything inclusive. God was so pleased with Noah that he renounced His curse on the earth and said no more will He curse the ground or destroy the earth through flood. The rainbow was His sign for that covenant, Genesis 8:20-22. The Noah's event gave birth to my dissertation that all questions, all problems, have scriptural promised answers and scripturally promised solutions. The What, the How and the Why of the Bible will guide you to locate and apply these promises. Always listen to God's signature tune, and always listen to the promptings of the Holy spirit. The Holy spirit is the voice of God. Noah was blessed with some modification from that of Genesis 1:28. Now he can eat the animals and the fear of him and the dread of him shall be on his enemies. Genesis 9:1-4. The only striking issue was that blood will be used to pay for blood. God's covenant was established Genesis 9:12-14. Noah's drunkenness resulted in his cursing one of his boys, Ham. As the population started coming up, evil started pilling up, and layers upon layers of evil that could not be tolerated. The straw that broke the camel's back, was the building of the tower of Babel. These rebels decided to build a tower that will reach Heaven so that they can no longer be scattered since their language was one and the expectations and imagination one. The power of imagination when used negatively or with wrong motives attracts immediate and devastating consequences as shown in Genesis 11:1-9; a big lesson of the consequences of disobedience.

The unity of the whole earth and the power of their imagination threatened even God and the Trinity had to come down to see what they had constructed in their imagination. This shows the power of imagination which we don't use often. Only in two places in the bible do we see positive use of imagination, all others are negatively applied and this Genesis 11:1 is a typical example where you see the immediate reply of Trinity to this negative motive application of imagination. Genesis 11:6. And the Lord said, behold the people are one and they have one language and now nothing will be restrained from them which they have imagined to do. So, what God did, how He did it and why He did it created a new lifestyle for the earth, different cultures, languages, different tunes. For now, when one speaks you can easily identify the region or tribe the individual hails from. All this is shown in Genesis 11:6-9, as evil continued to rise God had to come with another strategy to rescue mankind and save human race. God's good intention has been to restore the dignity of man. "Murray reminds us that in the Garden of Eden two ways were set before Adam and Eve for attaining the likeness of God, two ways typified by the two trees, the tree of life, and the tree of the knowledge of good and evil. God's way was that through life would come the knowledge and likeness of God. But Satan assured Adam that it was through knowledge that man may be like the Most High. Ever since then it has been difficult for men to put knowledge in its rightful place" (Lebar 1995, 151). There is a lot to be explained here and I will be dealing with what the trees represent, the allegory as I go on in stages till the completion, since it has been a case of war of words from Genesis to Revelation.

Chapter 4
Evangelism Started with Abram

Education was necessary and requires a drawn-out process. Abram was approached by God and the evangelism of Abram, a moon worshiper started off. All that God demonstrated was what He said and did, how He said it and did it, and Why He said it and did it. God is saying to us to use the examples He has shown us. Why do we find it difficult to learn, understand or acknowledge God despite His revealing himself to us? We have neglected what He has been saying and doing and How He has been saying it and doing it and Why He has been saying it and doing it all these years. The purpose of the dissertation is to highlight these deficiencies in our study of the Bible. Remember that God uses people, circumstances and events to reach out. Satan also uses people, circumstances and events to pervert God's plans, intentions and purposes. God's preaching education, revelations upon revelations to reveal Himself to Abram took some time. There were interruptions from within and without for Abram. Lot, his relation was a problem.

It was after the Tower of Babel episode, and the death of Abram's father, Terah in Haran, that God called Abram to move out of his country and from his relatives to a place He will show him. As stated in Genesis chapter 12 of KJV footnote, "God now turns our attention from rebellious humanity recently scattered by the judgement of Tower of Babel, to this one family through which the savior of the world would ultimately come". Here again, God told Abram His intentions as stated in Genesis 12:1-9. That is what He will do, How He will do it and why He will do it His way. Abram obeyed but this movement as I recall it inadvertently included Lot, Abram's kindred. God provided an answer to the problem of famine that occurred by directing Abram to Egypt. Even though Abram obeyed God, his faith to trust God was shaky as He was tested by events and circumstances in Egypt. Abram thought he could manipulate the issues, but here again, God weighed in and instead of Abram being punished, He was let go by Pharaoh untouched. Abram left Egypt for Canaan with his entourage. Both Abram and Lot were rich, very rich in cattle, in silver, and in gold, Genesis 13:2. This is an irony of history. The unseen problem created by Abram in travelling out with Lot did put on hold God's intimacy with Abram. The issue of prosperity had to be used to separate these two rich relatives. Genesis 13:10-13. It was after this separation that God's intimacy with Abram resumed. Unfortunately, Lot choice ended him on the side of Sodom, and sooner than later battle of kings occurred where Lot and family were taken captives, Genesis 14:12. Abram had to go to rescue his relative Lot and family which resulted in Abram being connected to Melchizedek. Abram demonstrated his unselfish character and ended up been blessed by Melchizedek a type of Jesus. This issue is covered in Genesis 14:1-24, and again illustrates that for every problem we face, God has an answer, and in this case, God was dealing with Abram based on His intentions for him, which is evangelism at its best.

Chapter 15 of Genesis dealt with God's relationship with Abram. Here God reveals to Abram His intentions. What He intends to do with Him and through Him, How He was going to do it and the why of it all. The striking issue here is in Genesis 15:6. Abram believed in the Lord and He counted it to him for righteousness. So evangelization of Abram started, the promises, the covenant, and the prophesies of the future all made known to Abram. The picture here is that in all these issues, the biblical promised answers to the questions were already in place and biblical promised solutions to the problem were already established. What was Abrams response but to co-operate and collaborate with God's plans, often with detached willingness.

Even though Abram believed in God, yet the acts of anxiety displayed brought more harm to the ugly situation which Abram went through. Yet as Abram deviates, God adjusts. Sin was still on the increase and yet sin was not being imputed in people's accounts. Psalm 32:2, "Blessed is the man unto whom the Lord imputed not iniquity and in whose spirit, there is no guile".

Sin was taken for granted and the lifestyle of people were deteriorating fast. Abram was the first person to be referred to as a Hebrew and was the forefather of both the Jews and the Arabs. God's pursuit for restoration must continue unabated. Abram brought more problems than expected, yet God's capability, availability and willingness to fulfill his promises to Abram couldn't be compromised. Every question that showed up had an answer and every problem had a solution. But one thing must be known and acknowledged. Sin must be paid for, for God to be God of justice.

"God's Grace is revealed in His providing an atonement whereby He could both justify the ungodly and yet vindicate His holy unchangeable law" (Pearlman 2007, 234). What happens when we ignore the What, the How and the Why of God? Just like Prof. Millard Erickson alluded in his book Christian Theology page 455, God is not necessarily punishing the offender in this case Abram, but that like in Abram's case, those acts of disobedience may set in motion a chain of adverse effect as in this case with Abram and Sarai, and may delay the plan of God like it surely did.

(1) Abram by default married Hagar and brought in Ishmael outside the will of God.

(2) God's promise must come to pass, but for now put on hold.

(3) The Almighty God has an answer and when the time comes His plans, and purposes must be fulfilled accordingly.

(4) The covenant requirements were reached with circumcision, name changes Sarai to Sarah and Abram to Abraham.

(5) These details are there in Genesis chapter 16 to chapter 21.

(6) God was still faithful to His promises to Abraham.

(7) Isaac arrived with Ishmael still on the scene.

(8) The relationship between Hagar and Sarah was rocky and Sarah had to tell Abraham to move out Hagar since the child of promise cannot share the inheritance. Abraham had to do that but begged God to bless Ishmael as well, which God did.

(9) Hagar and Sarah represented two covenants.

Covenant of law represents Hagar in Mount Sinai and Sarah's Covenant of Grace in Mount Zion. It's an allegory used in Galatians 4:21-24. Paul's argument against Judaism. The second allegory concerns the two trees in the garden which represents two foundations. The tree of life, Genesis 3:22, represents one foundation and the tree of knowledge of good and evil, Genesis 2:17, represents the second foundation which will be dealt later.

God had to test Abraham's willingness to obey to completion, by telling him to offer Isaac as a sacrifice. Abraham willingly obeyed without telling his wife Sarah. I am sure that if Abraham had told the wife, may be Abraham could've been accused or even tried for an attempted murder. God after seeing that Abraham meant business provided him with a substitute. Isaac was the type of Jesus who will be sacrificed for our sins. Abraham's obedience was validated by his willingness to obey to completion. When God stopped Abraham from sacrificing his son, God instructed him to turn to his right and use the substitute God had supernaturally provided, the lamb. Only God knew how and why Abraham and Isaac were there and He alone knows how to get them out from there, without any disappointments on either side. In response to Abraham's act of diluted faith God still promised to restore whatever Adam and Eve lost in the garden. This made Abraham the vital figure in the biblical redemption of mankind, being made the recipient to the promise of his descendants becoming a nation through him.

When it was time for Isaac to marry, Abraham sent his servant to go to his kindred to get a wife for Isaac. Rebecca was married and this is covered in Genesis 24. Isaac's wife Rebecca gave birth to Esau and Jacob. Even though Esau was the first and favorite of the father yet Jacob was Rebecca's favorite. This selective love characterization played out unfavorably in most families. Esau sold his birthright to his junior brother Jacob, because of hunger using a pot of porridge. So, the seed of enmity was sown and that sin of omission or commission is still floating around. Rebekah aided and abated the crime. God's intention was that since both the Nation of Israel and the expected church were to be modelled after the biblical family structure that the spirit of sonship should be developed. The anticipated spiritual parenting family again was disrupted and twisted.

God's covenant with Isaac was confirmed in Gen 26:1-5. His desire to move down to Egypt because of famine ended up at Gerar with Abimelech posing as a stumbling block. But here again God intervened and the whole episode ended in a covenant between Isaac and Abimelech Genesis 26:26-33. Esau was at the other end getting married to a Hittite which grieved Isaac and Rebekah. Jacob continued hiding from his brother Esau for years while God continued moving per His divine schedule, Gen 27:41. Jacob was warned not to marry from the daughters of Canaan, but should marry from the daughters of Leban, the mother's brother. Jacob a deceiver was deceived, what you sow you reap. Jacob ended marrying Rachel and Leah. The twelve sons of Jacob formed the twelve tribes of Israel with ten in the Northern Side. Israel with Samaria as the capital and Judah Southern part with Jerusalem as the capital. Jacobs favorite wife Rachel only gave birth to two sons, Joseph and Benjamin. Her maid, Bilhah, Rachel's handmaid, gave birth to Dan and Naphtali. Leah gave birth to six sons and a daughter Diana. The maid Zilpah, gave birth to two other sons Gad and Asher.

Chapter 5
God's Relationship with Joseph

Joseph's life was resembled the life of Jesus. Both were hated, sold by relatives for cash. Jesus later sacrificed Himself to save us and brought grace and truth. Joseph saved the people of Israel from famine but paid later for their disobedience when Pharaoh that knew not Joseph, nor the history behind Egypt's prosperity and civilization came to power. Jacob latter reconciled with his brother, Esau Gen 32. Jacobs name was changed after his encounter with God at Peniel, Gen 32:28. Joseph's story is given here in Genesis from chapter 37 to the end of Genesis 50. Joseph was prosperous although he was a slave. What happened, how it happened and why did it happen, shows what the dissertation is for, that for every issue in one's life, there is biblical promised answers to questions and biblical promised solutions to every problem that crops up. The lessons from Joseph makes an important event in history where God's provisions protection was on display and they are written down for us to use and avoid the hard knocks that follow when unknowns arise.

Joseph was called a dreamer and all sorts of names by his brothers who hated him because he was their father's favorite. They could have killed him if not for Reuben and Judah, who suggested that instead of killing him, they should accept his being sold as a slave to the Ishmaelites going to Egypt. Joseph by twist of events ends up in Potiphar's house and yet the Lord was with Joseph and he prospered. Even though Joseph escaped the knocks of slavery, yet (like the Barbarians of Melita who assumed Paul to die in Acts 28:4- 5) the ungodly false love of Potiphar's wife didn't allow Joseph to rest, expecting Joseph to comply to her request, which Joseph did not. Joseph was later falsely accused by Potiphar's wife and thrown into prison. Joseph didn't complain, didn't contend, but left his case in the hand of God. This is a lesson to be noted. God was quietly and gently preparing Joseph there in the prison, for the unexpected promotion. There is a 'there' for obedient people, Elijah experienced this 'there' during his lifetime, 1st Kings 17:4. Joseph's ability to interpret dreams positioned him for Pharaoh appointing him Second in Command, Gen 41:40. This event of Joseph, Potiphar's wife, the jail people, the chief butler, the baker, is covered by Genesis 39 to 41. Joseph's interpretation of Pharaoh's dream, exposed him and finally positioned him for appointment as Pharaoh's second in command. This shows and confirms the biblical saying in 2nd Timothy 3:12, "yea, and all that will live godly in Christ Jesus shall suffer prosecution". Pharaoh said to Joseph, "thou shall be over my house and according unto thy word shall all my people be ruled: only in the throne will I be greater than thou", Genesis 41:40. Joseph went from prison to palace. This illustrates our relationship with God especially when you obey to completion. God wants us to dwell with Him in other to serve Him. You cannot serve God from a distance. God is a spirit and those who worship Him must do so in spirit and in truth, John 4:24. God is steadily moving forward with His agenda despite distractions. Are you willing and obedient to follow him and obey and honor His instructions to bring glory to Him? Are you willing to become what God has created you to be?

The seven years of plenty is come and is gone and then the seven years of famine had set in. Joseph by God's divine plan built stores for Egypt to store grains that will last throughout the period of the famine. Egypt was feeding and supplying the entire known world with food. Joseph's reconciliation with the brothers started. The family of Israel was sent to Egypt to buy food. Joseph recognized his brothers (whom I am sure he was looking out for) who had treated him so badly with even attempted murder had it not been for God. They are now in the presence of their brother assumed dead, not knowing the providence of God at work and forgotten dreams revealed to them by Joseph. After dribbling them for some time and probing to see whether there is any change in their attitude and behavior, Joseph decided to reveal his identity to his brothers by speaking their language and showing them that he belonged to them by blood and by traditional circumcision. The brothers were shocked, and almost frozen with fear. Joseph then sent means to bring the entire family over to Egypt for settlement. Jacob got a word from God promising him not to fear and that he should go down to Egypt. Israel obeyed and went to Egypt. Pharaoh received them well and directed that they settle in the land of Goshen because the Egyptians abhor shepherds. Jacob and the family prospered in Goshen and Israel died there and was accordingly buried in Canaan. Pharaoh permitted Joseph to take the journey for his father's burial per Israel's culture and tradition. Jacob prophesied concerning his sons before his death, stating in Genesis 49:10. That is "the scepter shall not depart from Judah nor the lawgiver from between his feet until Shiloh come: and unto him shall the fathering of the people be".

Joseph lived in Egypt for a long time and before he died declared to his people in Genesis 50:25-26, saying, "God will surely visit you and ye shall carry up my bones from hence". So, Joseph died being a hundred and ten years old and they embalmed him and he was put in a coffin in Egypt. The people of Israel were starting to be treated as slaves when Pharaoh who didn't know Joseph appeared on the scene and saw how fast the Israelites were prospering in their own land. There were a lot of jealousy and this takes us to the exit of Abraham and arrival of Moses, God appointed deliverer as prophesied to Abraham years back, Genesis 15:14. And that nation whom they serve, will I judge and afterwards shall they come out with great substance. God is still God and no creation is without an open door for any type of escape in times of problem, 1st Corinthians 10:13. Where there is a problem, there is a promised solution and where there are questions there are scriptural promised answers. Where you find Pharaoh, you will see a Moses, Naomi, you will see Ruth. God's 'How' to get in and get out are always available. The death of Abraham is recorded in Genesis 25:5-11. In verse 5, Abraham gave all that he had to his promised son Isaac and to the other sons from his concubines, he gave gifts and sent them away from Isaac his son. It was after these events that Abraham died and was buried accordingly by his sons, Isaac and Ishmael.

The blessing of Joseph's sons is the one act among all others that the writer of Hebrews selected as an act of faith, Hebrew 11:21. God went into indoctrinating people like Isaiah the prophet to start speaking to Israel referring to the principle which God used to progressively reveal doctrine in scripture. Like my dissertation is based on 'what', 'how' and 'why' of the scriptures, Isaiah is setting out the answers to the questions and solutions to our problems. So, Isaiah 28:9-13 explains the what God said and did. How he did what he said and why He also did them. It's a process and it took time. From Adam to Moses, approximately a period of 2500 years, there were no written word or recorded revelation of God in scripture. The promises of redemption were in the hearts and mouths of the patriarchs and it must be remembered that God inspired Moses to write the Pentateuch, Exodus 34:27.

Why did God instruct Moses to write and record these Jewish experiences? One of the reasons could be found in the foot notes of 1st Corinthians 10:11 KJV. One of the reasons God caused Moses to record the experiences of the children of Israel was that He had Paul and the Corinthians believers in mind. He knew that the Corinthians were going to face similar crisis situations. When that time comes the example of the children of Israel would provide the deterrent to guide them from sin to lead them to spiritual victory. The children of Israel are now being used by God to demonstrate who He is, His capability, availability and willingness to handle their needs and their concerns. Kevin J. Conner wrote that "God communicated His mind and words in Old testament times by signs, shadows, types, examples, figures, allegory, dreams and visions, angelic manifestation and prophetic voice" (Conner 1982, 12). Many people have written concerning the acts of God but with scanty emphasis on How these promises, provisions, could be received. My dissertation lays emphasis on How we can locate these hows in the scripture and live the abundant life that John 10:10 promised. Just like the NLT study bible has said in Jonah 2:8, "that those who worship false god's, turn their backs on all God's mercies". Learn how to avoid that, by learning what God said and did. How he did what he said, and why He said and did it all. To round it up, Dr. Kevin J Conner emphasized that every practicing Christian believer should remember, and realize that "All doctrine must arise out of and be founded firmly upon, the only absolute authority in man's possession, the inspired and infallible word of God" (Conner 1982, 12). This takes us into Part 2, the arrival of Moses on the scene. What did Moses do? how did he do it and why did he do it? We will see and learn what tune he was dancing to, listening or hearing with his heart.

PART TWO

Moses and Pharaoh: Before and After Mount Sinai

Chapter 6

Pharaoh trains his enemy

This part concerns Moses showing up on the scene. God is a good God who plans His acts ahead of time. Moses who is to deliver Israel is being raised in the enemy's house, fed and nourished by the enemy, nursed and brought up by his biological mother, all this unknown to Pharaoh of Egypt and his household. All they know is that he is the child of Pharaoh's daughter. With Moses stepping into the scene God once more tells us what He is going to do with Moses. How He is going to direct Moses and why He God will do it that way. That is God's signature tune coming to be established in Old Testament period.

The starting point starts before the birth of Moses, the Jewish people whom God has set apart as his own people on earth were in Egypt now, suffering under the Pharaoh that knew not Joseph because of their rebellious attitude. Nothing could stop them. They were even intermarrying with the Egyptians which God was against it. Misconduct was rampant that people lost all forms of decency, conscience and godly behavior was a thing of the past. God has a plan. A plan to restore the dignity of man. A plan to restore His people Israel and still use them as an example to the world. God has revealed Himself to Moses through the burning bush incident. The man Moses is said to have brought law and order and that grace and truth came by Jesus Christ. John 1:17. Before this time the only law known was the law concerning the affairs in the garden of Eden in which God told Adam in Genesis 2:16-17 "of every tree of the garden thou mayest freely eat, but of the tree of the knowledge of good and evil, thou shall not eat of it, for in the day that thou eatest thereof, thou shall surely die." Without the law, the knowledge of sin will not be manifest and Satan could not have tempted Adam and Eve. As sin was not imputed to anyone's account, people were doing whatever they liked.

Moses birth showed clearly the signature tune of God showing what He said and did, how He said it and did it and why He said it and did it. Pharaoh sent out a decree in Exodus I:22 commanding the midwives and giving them, instructions saying," every son that is born by Hebrew parents, ye shall cast into the river and every daughter ye shall save alive" God had already made plans on how Moses will be saved, nursed nurtured and trained for the purpose for which God created Him. The problem is our belief system that went down with Adam in the garden, conscience replaced love and since then it has been a struggle for mankind. Questions without answers and problems without solutions. But we forget to remember that there are spiritual as well as scriptural promised answers and solutions to our problems respectively.

To so many people, Moses caused Israel's prolonged stay in Egypt beyond God's calendar for the transition because of Moses' anxiety to jump-start his assignment. Moses having been raised by his biological mother, had some knowledge of who he is and had some idea of God's assignment regarding God's people. His miscalculation and wrong timing resulted in His premature exit to the wilderness for almost forty years adding more years to Israel's bondage in Egypt. But when you look at what happened next you will see that when you stay prepared, you wouldn't be unprepared. Moses needed that wilderness experience for what was ahead.

The burning bush experience was God's call on Moses for the journey to start. When Moses turned to listen to God's voice, God stepped in with the what, how and why you are there. This reminds me of the statement by Eckhart Tolle saying, "You are here to enable the divine purpose of the universe to unfold; that is how important you are" (Tolle 1999, VII). All of Moses's questions were answered and all the problems both anticipated and expected had solutions already; Exodus 3:9-22. God strengthened Moses more by turning his shepherd's rod to become God's rod. The answers were there and the solutions were already on display before the problems arose; Exodus 4:1-13. Moses is being trained and equipped for the Job.

Moses and Aaron's first encounter with Pharaoh was stormy and thus Israel's labor was tripled that the people of Israel started blaming Moses for their hardship, saying that they should have been left alone. But God did remember His promise and covenant with their ancestors Abraham, Isaac and Jacob. Nothing can prevent the promise being fulfilled no matter what. When the operation started, God was dishing out punishments and exposing the limitations of Pharaoh and exposing his inability to challenge God's authority. The snake of Moses swallowing Pharaoh's snakes, the ten plagues and Pharaohs responses were all noted and observed by Pharaoh's magicians. Pharaoh's magicians had no answers than to attribute what was happening to the finger of God, Exodus 8:19. It is said that Pharaoh's hearts was hardened. When you look at it, you will notice by scriptural interpretation that failure to consider God's words, His miracles, resulted in Pharaoh's heart being hardened. What you fail to consider will harden your heart, Mark 6:52, for they considered not the miracle of the loaves for their hearts were hardened. In the same token Pharaoh after seeing the miracle of Moses, failed to yield to God's divine power resulted in hardness of his heart. Each time he ignores the miracles and the effects on his subjects, His heart hardens; Pharaoh had no conscience, Exodus 8:19. To crown it all the Lord brought it to an end with the death of every first born of Egypt including their animals.

Chapter 7
A New Pharaoh

The exit of the Israelites from Egypt gave birth to the Passover feast, Exodus 12:1-28, hence reaffirming God's provision and protective promises to Israel in Exodus 23:20-23. When you look at what is happening, how it is happening, you will see the why it is happening. Moses needed some knowledge of the wilderness, since the Israelites were going to spend some number of years in the wilderness. You must have been there or have experienced what you will lead people through. Like Jonah, he came out from his rebellious attitude to preach to rebellious people of Nineveh. As such he knew what he went through about God's plans to complete His purpose.

God means what He says and says what He means. "God is not a man, that he should lie, neither the son of man, that he should repent: hath he said, and shall he not do it? Or hath he spoken, and shall he not make it good?", Numbers 23:19. God will not permit your leading people where you have not been to. Nothing you are going through in life will be a waste as God will use it, as and when due to bring you to your destiny. Even though Moses anxiety caused Israel to over stay in Egypt for several years, yet it wasn't a wasted adventure. It was a training period for Moses to study the wilderness as he will lead the Israelites through there. The day now arrives; this is the last of the Romans to go. All the first sons of the Egyptians including first born animals must die because of Pharaoh's stubbornness and arrogance.

Angels that will carry out the operation were to Passover the doorposts of the Israelites at seeing the blood. This is still observed as one of Israel's feasts. Instructions were given about the Passover lamb. The lamb shall be without blemish, a male of the first year. At the end of the exercise, Pharaoh was compelled to let the Israelites move out of Egypt. The Israeli women had to go to every household of Egypt, demanding jewelries. They spoiled the Egyptians and left for 11 days' journey as plotted. About 3 million people left Egypt for the Promised Land. Apart from Joshua and Caleb, none of the original Israelites that left Egypt entered the Promised Land, Numbers 14:26-35. Israelites were not willing to work with God and take instructions. They were not willing to become what God had created them to be.

What is demonstrated throughout this journey is that for every question asked, there is a scriptural promised solution. Session after session, event after event, God is assuring us of His capability, availability, and willingness to meet our needs. How we position ourselves to receive these promises is all in the bible. God is always telling us what He has done, how He did it and why. It takes the 'How' of God to be successful or to stand differently. We must start paying attention to the 'Hows' of the Bible. The receiving of the word consists in two parts; attention of the mind and intention of the will, said one William Ames.

During the Passover God gave them instructions to follow, the ordinance of the Passover. They were fully informed on what to do, how to do it and why they are doing it. This is how God speaks, and that's His signature tune. Moses knew too well how to dance to that tune. David was an excellent dancer to that tune and God said that David was a man after his heart. How and what did they do during the night's journey to the Promised Land? Where did they buy clothes, food? etc. God took care of these before they even thought of them. This is the beginning of the "seek you first the kingdom of God" stated in Mathew 6:33. The pillar of cloud guided them during the day and the pillar of fire by night. When the pillar starts moving the Israelites will move with it. Our responsibility is to be willing to obey and trust God's instructions and follow God's appointed leaders. The problems that showed up along the road were secretly, silently, and miraculously handled. Shortage of drinking water was sorted out when God made water break forth from a rock. Exodus 17:6. Despite all the ways that God showed and demonstrated his capability, availability and willingness in the wilderness, yet the Israelites weren't impressed. After the defeat of the Amalekites, Moses' in-law Jethro advised Moses on how to govern, regarding the distribution of responsibilities to other men of integrity amongst them. Despite all efforts, the rebellious attitude of Israelites continued unabated. With the Israelites, it was not the broken relationship that continued, but the broken fellowship that persisted. Faith has no song when fellowship is broken, Psalm 137:1-6. Jethro's advice gave rise to the appointment of judges and the judiciary system we have now but these days with judges who have little or no fear of the Lord.

How did the people of Israel cross the sea of Reeds, that is the Red Sea? Can anyone guess how they were going to cross that sea? There were cries, tears were rolling down their cheeks like rivers. The questions looked as if no answers were coming. You have the questions but God has the answers, you have the problems God has the solutions to your every need. The only thing Moses assured them was that if they can stay still and hold their peace that they will see the salvation of God, Exodus 14:12-14. It was after the Israelites saw what God has said and done, How He did it and why He did it could they burst into joy. Their belief and their faith generated what I call the national anthem of Old testament Israelites and that is what you see in Revelation 4:11. "Thou art worthy, O Lord to receive glory and honor and power, for thou hast created all things and for thy pleasure they are and were created". This is the bible saying that faith without a corresponding action, is dead. What did put a new song in the mouth of these rebels as Moses once called them was the signature tune of God regarding what they have seen, experienced, saw how their enemies were destroyed, were they able to believe that God is the God of Israel and that produced the action that resulted in the singing and dancing. God is telling them to trust Him and like Dr. Creflo Dollar says during his TV sermon that trust is the currency of the kingdom. What God is teaching them and us here is that the action produced should be born out of our belief, and that is what the Bible means by faith without a corresponding act is dead, James 2:17. Let God be true but every man a liar, Romans 3:4.

Moses sang his own song which he wrote down in Exodus 15 and what did Miriam do in Exodus 15:21 but to sing with the people to the Lord, God of Israel. Both Moses and Miriam who sang with the others all sang that they will sing unto the Lord for he hath triumphed gloriously, the horse and his rider hath he thrown into the sea in keeping with Moses words of Exodus 14:13, "for these Egyptians whom ye have seen today, ye shall see them again no more forever". Who is like unto thee O Lord is normally the song that comes to mind. When God secretly, miraculously and supernaturally answers our questions and quietly settles our enemies. "I will sing to the Lord, because He has dealt bountifully with me. A covenant relationship with the living God transforms a song from a desperate cry for help to a victorious anthem of praise, or glorifying God and proclaiming His grace to others" (Reid 2014, 12). Miriam is regarded as a prophetess and a singer of God's praise in Exodus 15:20. As David Roper wrote "there is awesome power in silence, especially in those overwhelmingly bad situations in which we are subject to harsh words from those we love. Silence, I have come to believe, is the answer to many of life's contradictions, so I am learning to say less these days. Silence was often our Lord's way" (Roper 2008, 131). God's release of Israel as slaves in Egypt defined them as a nation in the book of Exodus, and event of their crossing the Red sea, established their identity as having a divine relationship with their God, the God of Abraham, Isaac, and Jacob. The elimination of Egyptian army by

God of Israel was noised over the known world and Rahab used the fear raised to her advantage during her encounter with the spies of Israel. The whole of Israel lost hope but Abraham didn't, and because he demonstrated a desire to glorify God and bring honor to him, he received clear instructions on how to cross the Red Sea.

Exodus Chapters 1 through 18, is all about God's grace on the people of Israel. That is God's unmerited, unearned and undeserved favor. God is about to show them who they are and tell them the naked truth. God is now going to show them what they have been enjoying unknown and unappreciated, their ingratitude and their stiff neck. Billy Graham said that ingratitude is a sin and I do agree with him. They are now at Mount Sinai. Here again God called on Moses and the signature tune sounds. Moses, this is what I am going to do, this is how I am going to do it and this why it must be done so. This is the turning point of history. Can the people of Israel handle this process? Can they believe and trust their God that have done so much for them? We will soon find out.

Chapter 19 is about the 'What' of the Bible. What God said and did, what God told Moses to tell the children of Israel and what their reply was. First remember and don't forget (Deuteronomy 9:7, Deuteronomy 29:1) deals with it all. For now, let's see how they replied to Exodus 19:4-6. God was reminding them the incidents, the events and the occurrences, telling them that they have seen what He did unto the Egyptians and how He bore you on eagle's wings and brought you unto myself. And now therefore, if ye will obey my voice (in other words dance to my tune) indeed and keep my covenant then ye shall be a peculiar treasure unto me above all people for all the earth is mine. And ye shall be unto me a kingdom of priests and a holy nation. These are the words which thou shall speak unto the children of Israel. Moses delivers God's request and requirement for the covenant and listen to the reply from the people verse 8. And all the people answered together and said. All that the Lord hath spoken we will do. And Moses returned the words of the people unto the Lord.

Acceptance speech. The How of the Lord showed up and Moses has to let the people know how to prepare for the 'Ifs' and thou shall not series. The Ten Commandments were given. May I ask? Why did God give them these commandments which totaled six hundred and thirteen in number including the ten commandments and with what we now know from what James said about the Law, if you break one you have broken the whole. James 2:10, "for whosoever shall keep the whole law and yet offend in one point, he is guilty of breaking them all". It follows from all indications that severe punishment is attached to any breaking of the law, a curse to be sure. Someone was stoned for gathering sticks on the Sabbath day Numbers 15:35. And if any mischief follows then thou shalt give life for life, Exodus 21:23.

Eye for eye, tooth for tooth, hand for hand and foot for foot, Exodus 21:24. Every detail was given about keeping the law and every punishment spell out for disobedience. Even disobedience to parents attracted death penalty by stoning. Israel was living by the law. In the Law of Moses, every how and why of the law was given. What was the law all about? God knew from the beginning that they cannot keep all the laws. They may pretend to be doing the keeping, but God knows they do not. The law as I have learned and have heard was to bring the Israelites to the end of themselves. To show them that they need a Savior, nothing more than that and nothing less than that. It is a question of, if you do this, God will do that. Self-effort, self-performance. All these led to pride, arrogance, jealousy, envy, and name it. Can they realize this and how long will it take them to believe and turn to God? Everything was done to assure Israel that God's concern for them was high. Moses did all he could to no avail. Moses the meekest man on earth was pushed to disobey God at some instances. The first rock God instructed Moses to strike for water to come out, Exodus 17:6. The second rock required just speaking the word for water to come out. In part God instructed Moses to speak unto the rock before the eyes of his people and it shall give water. Moses not only disobeyed but called the Children of God rebels in addition to striking the rock twice. For Moses punishment, God denied his compulsive leadership to take Israel into the Promised Land.

So, throughout Exodus, it was what God said what He instructed. Knowing fully well that they were not going to obey the law, God instituted that they make Him a Sanctuary that He may dwell amongst them, Exodus 25:8. This was what God advised so that the animal sacrifice could continue so that God will through that process cover their sins until the arrival of the Messiah. All instructions were given about the building of the tabernacle, the outer court the inner court and inner most court the holy of the holies. The table, the wood that is to be used, the candle stick, the tabernacle, the altar, the courts of the tabernacle, were to follow God's instruction. The oil for the lamp, the priest's garment, the priest breast plate, the rope, consecrating the priest, the altar of incense, the offering of the tabernacle, the laver, the oil and the perfume were all considered, including the appointment of the workmen. This is renewal of the covenant with Abraham, Isaac and Jacob. All these were carefully undertaken, including the construction of the ark of covenant. The priest does represent the people before God. The animal sacrifice for Israel was to be done once a year and it was that if the priest is good the whole of Israel will be ok, if bad all will be labelled bad. Remember now that the word of God is an authority, an example, a law, a covenant, a dispensation, a favor, a promise, and the truth. For now, we must be aware of the moral laws of God and adhere strictly to what has been said, and how it is said and why it is said.

The book of Leviticus is all about the How of God. The way to wholeness. This book of Leviticus is to me one of the very important books of the Bible. The most striking issue in the How of Leviticus is seen in Leviticus 20:26 which says, "and ye shall be holy unto me for I the Lord am holy and have severed you from other people that ye should be mine". I have separated you, set you apart for my purpose. The prophets started declaring God's purpose, starting with Isaiah 14:24-27, which states, "The Lord of hosts hath sworn, saying, surely as I have thought, so shall it come to pass, and as I have purposed, so shall it stand. That I will break the Assyrian in my land, and upon my mountains tread him under foot, then shall his yoke depart from off them, and his burden depart from off their shoulders. This is the purpose that is purposed upon the whole earth, and this is the hand that is stretched out upon all the nations. For the Lord of hosts hath purposed, and who shall disannul it? And his hand is stretched out, and who shall turn it back?"

Holiness speaks of wholeness, nothing missing not broken. The only one thing God needs from us is our co-operation and collaboration as I earlier mentioned. A lot have been written about purity but until we embrace the how it's done, dance to the tune of God can we be able to let what Hebrew 10:23 said and I quote, "let us hold fast the profession of our hope without wavering (for He is faithful) that promised". "When Adam came from God he was perfect and whole, nothing missing and nothing broken. He bore the beauty and splendor of the image and the likeness of God. He was functioning like God intended humanity to function" (Stedman 2005, 13). We always tell people to do this and do that without telling them how to scripturally do it. To let practicing Christians who believe, to allow their belief to generate the action needed for the job to be done and be sure we do and act as we ought to do. Let your belief generate the divine healing and your faith produce the corresponding action needed. As I mentioned earlier, let your action be born out of your belief system, out of your trust, and out of the gift of faith of Christ. Speak what you believe and believe what you speak.

By doing this, we prevent the ugly influences others have on us. When we look at the Bible you can at once see, listen and read the signature tune of God. You observe his what, how and why by turning off other tunes. In Mathew's write-up on the beatitudes of Matt 6: 31-33, he stressed the How of God. But seek ye first the kingdom of God and his righteousness, and all these other things shall be added unto you. This means seek you How the kingdom works. Seeking How the kingdom works is based on What God has said about the kingdom, and the why behind His saying. This is how you discover the scriptural promised answers to your questions and the scriptural promised solutions to your problems. Many writers including Ray. C. Stedman have commented that "we are so quick to reverse God's priorities. We spend most of our time and energy thinking about how to get money to provide food and clothing and so on and we leave hardly any time for what God considers the essentials. No wonder our lives are frequently out of order" (Stedman 2005, 193). Ray Stedman also goes on to say that "God calls us to put our lives back in balance" (Stedman 2005,193). This is the 'How', which we as Christians have ignored and still ignoring. The Bible says, how can we escape mistakes, failures, if we ignore the 'What' of God, the 'How's' and 'Whys' of God and continue dancing the tune of the World using World means to meet godly requirements. How can we escape poverty? What 'Poor' means in analysis: P(Pass) O(Over) O(Opportunities) R (Repeatedly / Repetitively). Passing over opportunities repeatedly. God is telling us 'How' to do it His way and avoid the hard knocks of going through the ugly experiences. Learn from the experiences of others and the divine examples found in the scriptures. In spite of all the machinery, set in place to convince and convict the people of Israel, they continued to mess up. The law which was given to be their teacher couldn't help much. Leviticus ended showing all the available 'Hows' that could have helped Israel to turn completely to God. Instead they were drawn to the world system calling for a king to help them out.

Ray C. Stedman's explanation of our seeking first the kingdom of God in Matthew 6:31-33 was clearly understood pointing out to the fact that God had already provided scriptural promised answers to our questions and scriptural promised solutions to our problems, but because of our being so quick to reverse God's priorities we miss it all together. We are not doing it correctly and that's what my dissertation is trying to point out. As Ray. C. Stedman points out; "He sets aside so much for love, so much for joy, so much for peace, forgiveness, companionships understanding and guidance. These are the essentials as God sees them" (Stedman 2005, 193). But we are seeing it from a different angle. This is How we do things God's way by doing it as God has intended it to be done. This is most striking because many of us are not practicing Christianity like the Israelites were practicing the Law of Moses especially after Moses was gone. The pride and the sense of superiority kept the law so much alive and the ungodly benefits were so attractive and couldn't be ignored.

Ray C. Stedman commented on Leviticus 17 and 18, that "two areas of life were particularly regulated for the people of Israel -- their behavior towards blood and their behavior towards sex" (Stedman 2005, 208). The Bible is saying that because the life of every creature is its blood, humans should avoid consuming the blood. Here I can, only agree that many Christians are not strictly Christians probably because they are not practicing Christianity the way God intended it to be practiced and because we forget to embrace salvation alone without acknowledging redemption the way it was intended to be. So, when you look at what is happening in Christendom you will notice that many have no idea what correctly God has said and done. How he said it and did it, what He has done and of course why He has done it so. We also all concur to the fact that with God all things are possible and that God is love and love is God. So, in spite of all these explanations we still do not agree that there are scriptural promised answers to our questions and scriptural promised solutions to our problems. Study the bible, read books written by inspired scholars of the Bible and you will see the difference. It takes courage to be different, so says T.D. Jakes, but for me, it takes the How of God to be successful. When you remember, and don't forget what God has said and done, How He said it and did it and why he said and did it you will find the answers and solutions which are very much at your disposal. Maybe it's time to dump political correctness and start adopting biblical correctness.

When we misplace our values, we misplace our lives. When we do this, we find ourselves on the defensive mood and no longer on the offensive. We simply believe in others to understand through revelation, illumination and inspiration of others and not ours. When people read the Bible, study it, but fail to apply it for making course corrections in one's life, it's just like eating without digesting. Leviticus advised that we move in life with God's moral agenda. We need to personalize our relationship with God and rely on His promises, 2nd Corinthians 1:20-22, Hebrew 10:23.

Chapter 8

Moses the Deliverer

In Numbers, the Bible teaches preparations in the Wilderness covering their years in the wilderness, Chapter 1-26. They left Mount Sinai still complaining and murmuring but this time they must pay for it. Moses got a signal from God ordering that spies be sent to spy the land probably to see how far the land's status quo flowing with milk and honey. Expose them and activate them for action. The story of this event and the consequences is covered in the book of Numbers chapters 13 and 14.

The report brought back by these spies were troubling and apart from Caleb and Joshua the report was devastating. Numbers 13:30-33 were horrible to the ear. You could easily see the power of imagination regarding how the ten saw themselves as grasshoppers and how the land eateth up the inhabitants. How are the mighty fallen? Caleb and Joshua rent their clothes in annoyance and the people even threatened to stone them. How can God intervene when you have already judged and sentenced yourself? Like Proverbs 23:7 said, "As a man thinketh in his heart so he is". Frustrated and disappointed they started making plans to appoint a captain to take them back to Egypt, Numbers 14:4. Despite the encouragement and assurance of Caleb and Joshua that God had already given them the land. How can they miss-out on God's promise to Abraham, Isaac and Jacob? The rebellion grew stronger and stronger. The dialogue between Moses and God is recorded in Numbers 14:11-38. God had to give the verdict and Moses must move on. Caleb and Joshua were spared of this verdict. Moses pleaded that God should temper justice with mercy and not forget the promises He made to Abraham, Isaac and Jacob. This issue is covered in Numbers 14:13-20. A lot of issues that cropped up were dealt with accordingly. When we ignore or neglect the What, the How, and Why of God, you are in for failure. When you fail to plan, you have planned to fail. Moses will always be remembered for his undiluted relationship with God and for God's respect for Moses whom He honored by withdrawing His anger to destroy Israel, Exodus 32:9-14. The two censuses break the book into two logical divisions. Chapters 1-21 begin with a census and cover the years in the wilderness while chapters 26-36 begins with census of the new generation and tells of the months before entrance into Canaan. Final touches were placed accordingly. Cities for Levities, cities of refuge and other issues were settled. The instruction you obey is the future you create. So, mind whose instructions you are willing to obey.

God's idea may not be substantiated scripturally, but one must go with it. We have all seen that this event really didn't go well with Israel. God's punishment on Israel was heavy. It was a mistake probably by Moses and all those layers of ugly events that really denied Moses the chance of stepping into the Promised Land, but who knows? All the laws concerning offerings, stoning of offenders and other acts of disobedience especially disobedience to God's anointed people were spelt out. It's said in the scriptures that we "touch not My anointed and do my prophet no harm", Psalm 105:15. God dealt with Israel's murmuring. All these are recorded for our own sake. All these show us what God did and how He did it and why He did it. God continues to show us all the provisions, the protection and His concerns. All arrangement was made with emphasis on the priest and Levites concerning the laws. In Numbers 18:6-7. God stated what He did, How He did it and why He did it. So, every question has a scriptural promised answer and every problem has a scriptural promised solution and the scriptures have all over how to access these promises; Ask, seek, knock, Luke 11:9. The knocking involves knocking down your fears, your unbelief and your doubts. To Adam and his family, it was a covenant of salt confirmed and established by God to Aaron and his seeds, Numbers 18:19.

As they draw to the end of this chapter murmuring and acts of disobedience even on part of Aaron and Moses continued to show up that Aaron was not even allowed to enter the Promised Land because of his disobedience against God's word at the water of Meribah. Eleazer, Aaron's son had to take-over from his father, after stripping Aaron of his garment and putting it on his son, Numbers 20:28. God used the murmuring and complaining to demonstrate the power of believing in Him. The murmuring and the complaining continued unabated, the people speaking against Moses and even God, reminding God and Moses again and again why they should have been left to die in Egypt and God again and again reminding them that there have been answers to their questions, solutions to their problems and here again God demonstrated His capability, his availability and His willingness to fulfill his covenant as established between Him and Abraham, Isaac and Jacob. Numbers 20:1 covered Miriam death Number's 20:2-13. One of the causes why Moses was denied entrance into the Promised Land. This is recorded in Numbers 20:8-12, Moses went over the call of duty and so angered God. This shows that obedience is highly valued in the sight of God. When we realize that Moses after all his being the meekest man on earth, and yet couldn't enter or lead the children of Israel into the promised land, you then can see what Christ's atonement did for us. What lessons have we so far learned from the journey so far? It's all about what, how and why of God. The most important issue is how we handle the what and why, which are always at each other's throat.

God because of Israel's continued rebellion despite all He has done for them, sent fiery serpents which did bite the people and many of them died, Numbers 21:4-9. Always a solution to their problem. When they complained, and repented for speaking against God and Moses, God directed Moses on what to do, how to do it and why it should be done as directed. This introduces the act of looking up to be saved and healed in Old testament, Numbers 21:8-9 and the act of believing in New Testament on the finished work of Jesus Christ, John 3:14-15, and be saved. "And as Moses lifted up the serpent in the wilderness even so must the son of man be lifted up, that whosoever believeth in Him should not perish, but have eternal life". The people of Israel experienced victories and failures, the error of Balaam telling us that no one has the right to curse whom God has blessed. No matter the circumstances it should not be done. God can use any means available to prevent this misleading by those He has called, Numbers 22:28-30 to perform. He used an ass to speak to Balaam. Here again, God revealed who He is, His signature tune, which is written down here in Numbers 23:19.

Despite all that transpired between Balaam and God, Balaam still deceived the people of Israel into committing sin, Numbers 25:1-5. The error of Balaam was a thorn in the flesh for the Israelites (Numbers 22:28) and had it not been for the zealousness of Phinehas for his God, shown by killing Zimri with the Midianite woman Cozbi. This could have landed Israel into another punishment, had this act not taken as an atonement for the people of Israel, which pleased God, Numbers 25:6-18. A lot was covered during this period before the arrangement for entering the Promised Land was completed. All the anticipated questions and solutions were discussed.

Chapter 26 dealt with the second numbering of the children of Israel from twenty years old and upwards. The record of the earth opening and swallowing up the Korah-Israelites are also written down and other occurrences like inheritance to be by lot, cities for the tribe of Levi, the law of inheritance and finally Joshua to succeed Moses. All the laws concluded including how the laws of vows should be taken, division of booty, how it should be shared. Moses last writing concerning the journey, laws concerning murder, cities of refuge, concerning bloodshed and female inheritance, marriage within the tribes. All these goes to show you that no stone was left unturned lending credit to God's signature tune. It was after all these explanations and discourse, What He did, How He did it and Why He did it, and then turned to Deuteronomy to conclude the Pentateuch. Disobedience to any of these concluded issues will attract a curse and constitute a sin against the Lord. You must be sure that your sin will find you out, Numbers 32:23.

Deuteronomy is the last recorded message of Moses before his death after which the Israelites prepared for entry into the promised land with Joshua. Moses concluded his mission with an address centered on the covenant laws. Here again it was what God has said, what he has done, How He said it and did it, why He said it and did it. Jesus even quoted a lot from Deuteronomy during his temptation Matthew 4: 1-11, Deuteronomy 6:13, 16, 8:3. Concerning the commandment Matthew 22:36-37 quoted Deuteronomy 6:5 from the write-ups Deuteronomy was the 5th most quoted in the new testaments and probably the 2nd most manuscripts apart from Psalms. Moses addressed Israelites recounting what God has said and done for them, how he delivered them and why He did what He promised. He mentioned why they spent so much time on the wilderness because of their rebellious attitude and warned that they should desist or face more punishment. He narrated their experiences right from Egypt through the wilderness and why the cities of refuge were established. Their covenant in Horeb in which they were all aware of, Deuteronomy 5:2-6, this included the Ten Commandments, a recap on it. He narrated how the first set of commandments were given to him and how they were broken and how and why the replacement was given. He told them what God required of them and explained in Deuteronomy

10:12-22. The greatness of God was completely explained. God's Signature Tune is expressed in chapters of the bible from Genesis to Revelation.

The blessings of the Promised Land were rehearsed and place of worship identified. You must not have any ungodly relationship with the occupants of the Promised Land. Isolate yourselves from them, no intermarriages should be allowed or worshipping their god's. Warning concerning idolatry which attracts death penalty was highlighted. Monetary issues were discussed. Three addresses were taken to enable him cover and recap all that have been instructed, confirmed and established. Finally, Moses must remind them that he has finished with what God had instructed him to do by his pronouncement and declaration of 6:7, 9:7, 28:1-13, 28:15-68, and 30:19. "I call heaven and earth to record this day against you, that I have set before your life and death, blessing and cursing, therefore choose life that both thou and thy seed may live". After all is said and done, Joshua was commissioned before the congregation with his statements of Deuteronomy 31:1-2 and Moses talked to Joshua in Deuteronomy 31:6 to be strong and of good courage and that he should not fear because God will always be there for him. Moses was like the father of the law and order. The law was like Moses' 'Will' and must be fully implemented after his death and that's exactly what happened.

Chapter 9

Recap – Events Before and After Joshua

At the end of it all, God told Moses to summon Joshua to the tabernacle of the congregation for divine commissioning. Moses along with Joshua followed the instruction as stated in Deuteronomy 31: 14-16 and 31:23 as the final charge to Joshua. After Moses has finished writing the law of what God said and did, How He did what he said and did and specially why he did it that he summoned all the elders and demanded that the law be put along with Aarons rod and Myrrah in the ark of the covenant for a witness against them as recorded in Deuteronomy 31:24-29. Moses also delivered his song to all the congregation of Israel mentioning among other things that his doctrine shall drop as the rain, his speech shall distill as the dew, this he spoke in the ears of the congregation of Israel the words of his song until they were ended, Deuteronomy 32:2. In closing he advised them to set their hearts unto all the words which he testified among them that day, which they have to instruct their children to observe, to do all the words of the law, Deuteronomy 32:46-47. Moses finally blessed all the tribes of Israel saying, "the eternal God is thy refuge and underneath are the everlasting arms, and he shall thrust out the enemy from before thee, and shall say, destroy them", Deuteronomy 33:27. Moses was a hundred and twenty years old when he died, his eyes were not dim nor his natural force abated, states the Bible, Deuteronomy 34:7. Moses walked to his grave and after God has shown him the Promised Land denied his entry. He died and only God identify where he is buried; and can tell, and He has not done so. In my conclusion, the book of Deuteronomy is all about, "remember and don't forget" what God has said and done, how He has said it and done it, why He said it and did it. So, God confirmed and established his statements, his order, his rank and authority, Deuteronomy 9:7.

Apply and practice God's inspired word, which when properly used and applied provides all we need for life and ministry, 2nd Timothy 3:14-17.

God is always willing to reward the overcomers. Abraham's belief in God and Moses belief in God is what is expected to produce or generate the corresponding response or actions that the Bible has been hammering about. My total observation to these first five books of the Bible is that there are to me two birthdays. There are also two estimations of our ages. God's estimation and human estimation. The physical birthday, the date your biological mother gave birth to you and the spiritual birthday, that is the day you become a 'Born again Christian', taking Jesus as your Savior, 2nd Corinthians 5:17.

In age, we look at our physical ages along with signs and wonders that go with it while God looks at our spiritual age and that to me probably was why Sarah and Abraham could get their son Isaac when they have passed the natural or physical age by our estimation on child-bearing age. Also, look at Moses who at one hundred and twenty years of age, going with his eyes not dim, nor his natural force abated, walking to his grave. When we put these two together and scripturally realize that as a thousand years in the sight of us are but as yesterday in God's Kingdom, your guess will be as good as mine in keeping us wondering and thanking God for His goodness, praising Him for His Greatness and worshiping Him for His wholeness and holiness. When you put the three scriptures that I made references to in my exposition/ preposition then you will be able to draw your own conclusion as to the wisdom of God and His divine calculations where for instance one plus one is one in marriage, Job 10:5, has this to say; Are thy days as the days of man? Are thy years as man's days? Before Moses died he warned the nation of Israel of the dangers of an incomplete conquest, with the resultant intercourse with the unbelieving pagan people of Canaan, Exodus 34: 11-16 and Deuteronomy 7:1-5. Moses' fears had already become a reality as a result of walking away from God's plan and purpose for him.

Psalms 90:4 has this to say: For a thousand years in thy sight are but as yesterday when it is past and as a watch in the night. "But, beloved, be not ignorant of this one thing that one day with the Lord as a thousand years and a thousand years as one day", 2nd Peter 3:8. All these go to show us that all things are possible with God and that all our questions have scriptural promised answers and all our problems have scriptural promised solutions. With these, to believe and trust God, becomes less troublesome as doubts, unbelief and fear are removed, from our system. This demonstrates Lord's goodness and faithfulness, which freely gives birth to repentance, Romans 2:4.

The book of Joshua opens a new horizon in the history of the Israelites. God intends to use His chosen nation to bless the world at large, acquaint them with the wisdom, knowledge and understanding of the true God and the Messianic messages. So, it's a record of God's faithfulness to his covenant people and traces the record of the children of Israel from the shores of the Jordan how he did it and why he did it has its root on how God constituted the entire nation of Israel, a kingdom of priests each member being recorded as being in touch with God and His holy tabernacle. As Myer Pearlman said, "Every Israelite was therefore holy, that is, set apart for God and every activity and sphere of his life was regulated by the law of holiness" (Pearlman 2007, 130). We must scripturally realize and be aware that God reveals himself to us through his names. "God has a name to meet the needs of any situation we may face in life" (Evans 2014, 15). Tony also stated "that in scripture, a name often connotes purpose, authority, make-up and character" (Evans 2014, 12). He goes on to say that name "routinely carries with it the idea of power, responsibility, purpose and authority." (Evans 2014, 12). The Power of God's Names, by Tony Evans explains God's use of His names to meet our needs and concerns. Evans said that "because of the depth of God's character, He has various names that reflect the many ways He related to humanity. For example, God is called Elohim when revealing Himself as the all-powerful Creator. He is Jehovah Nissi, the Lord's banner of victory. God is also known as Jehovah Rapha, the Lord your healer. When you need provision, get to know the name Jehovah Jireh, God the provider" (Evans 2014, 12).

Dr. Tony Evan continued that "when God is not properly understood, valued and appreciated for who He truly is, using His name is like an identity theft. To know God's names is to experience His nature, and that level of intimacy is reserved for those who humbly trust and depend on Him. God will not share His glory with anyone. We must realize our insignificance before we can recognize the significance that comes only through Him. We are to hallow His name and His name alone. You can't know His name until you forget your own" (Evans 2014, 18, 19).

I completely agree with him and when you match what he has so far said, with my dissertation concept, you will come to realize the love of God for his creation. You will come to be convinced that every individual whether or not she/he serves God, "is sustained by the creative power of God's spirit", Daniel 5:23, Acts 17:28" (Pearlman 2007, 291). The Bible is showing us that God does His things secretly, silently and supernaturally, all the time. When you believe and trust God, "He will come into your life and connect your problem with His solutions, your needs with His provision and your circumstances with His intentions, creating something brand new in you. If you want to discover your destiny, begin by embracing the truth that you were made on purpose for a purpose that lines up with God's intentions for you" (Evans 2013, 74). This is how God does His things assuring you of His concerns for His creation. He's a faithful God. Now that Moses has died the law which stands as the 'Will' will now be thoroughly and fully implemented, but the sacrifice continues, Exodus 20:24. All that Dr. Evans, Myer Pearlman, Dick Iverson, Prof M.J. Erickson, Dr. Roger E Olson, Dr. Gregg R Allison are all saying or writing is based on what God has said, and did, how he has said it and did it and why he has said it, which is God's signature tune. You start explaining or evangelizing with the Why and that was how the apologetic writers moved into explaining based on What God has said, promised, the examples that have been shown.

Joshua was called by God to let him know how to start, where to start and why he must start immediately. As we do observe, the Bible teaches and sets standards, and history confirms it. Joshua 1:8-9 has been a widely-used bible verse and even though we read it day in day out, implementing it has been a problem. It must go from the written to the living. Joshua 1:8, it is God speaking directly to Joshua; "this book of the Law shall not depart out of thy mouth, but thou shall mediate there in day and night, that thou mayest observe to do per all that is written therein, for then thou shalt make thy way prosperous and then thou shalt have good success". From Joshua 1-9, it's God talking to Joshua. The Whats, the Hows and the Whys of God clearly voiced to Joshua. God's signature tune having been revealed to Joshua signals it's time to move, the set time is now, the time to crossover to the other side. Joshua called his officers and addressed them as to what God has said and How He said it and Why He said it. Jordan must be crossed; the Promised Land must be secured and distributed accordingly. "This day have I rolled away the reproach of Egypt from off you wherefore the name of the place is called Gilgal unto this day", Joshua 5:9.

Two spies were sent to spy Jericho. They came back to report how Rahab a prostitute has helped them to escape and as such opening a door to divine connection. Jordan was crossed with all the undertakings and Jericho was taken per the promises of God. Rahab was compensated because of her conviction that the God of Israel was the only true God, Joshua 2:9-21. Rahab's story comes with illustration of God's signature tune. One may ask how?

(1) God positioned her divinely for the job which was to be assigned to her.

(2) God was exposing her to perform. She was positioned, exposed, being at the right place at the right time with the right attitude, 1st Corinthians 2:9.

(3) Rahab was bold to take risk for herself and the spies. She knew the consequences, if her deal was discovered but was ready to take it because she was convinced that Israel's God was the real God.

(4) She had the knowledge of history, Joshua 2:9-10, 2nd Peter 2:9 pertaining to what God had done for the Israelites, How He did it, and Why He did it, gave her courage to stand her ground on what she was convicted of.

God commanded Joshua on what to do when they have crossed Jordan again, showing that the entire Bible is replete with what God said, how He said it and why He said it. Here in Joshua 4:1-24, the Bible is telling us how and why of it, verse 6-8 said it all. First, that this may be a sign among you that when your children ask their fathers in time to come, saying, what mean you by these stones, the answer followed in verse 7 and how in verse 8. Before the fall of Jericho, Joshua was instructed to circumcise again the children of Israel before entering the city of Jericho, a covenant fulfilment, Joshua 5:5-6. The history of how Jericho wall came down after the 7th match around the city wall goes to portray the power of God. Seven in Jewish number meaning completion. A story of a man who went to a car dealer to buy a car was told by our Bishop Harry Jackson in my local church, Hope Christian Church of Beltsville Maryland, how a certain man made use of this divine means to accomplish his goal at a car dealership. They initially told him that his credit wasn't good enough to purchase the car. The man excused himself from them, went to that car, walked around the car seven times and came back to the dealer who told him he was not credit worthy originally to buy that car. The man went back and demanded a recheck on his credit and it was revealed at this time to be ok for him to buy the car. The man finally purchased the car and left. That's a good example of one's belief and trust that for every problem there is scripturally promised solutions. So, his trust on God's word left him laughing and smiling home with his car of choice. This in keeping with walking around Jericho wall 7 times that brought the walls down, per God's word. Those who believe and trust God will never be disappointed.

Rahab who saved the Israelites that spied the land reminded us of what God said to Noah in Genesis 9:2 and relating to Israel simply means the fear of Israel and the dread of Israel will be upon their enemies. Joshua's curse on Jericho. Joshua 6:26 was rectified by Elisha, in 2nd Kings 2:19-23 and Israel's promise to save Rahab honored by Joshua in Joshua 6:25. At the end of it all, Joshua like Moses addressed his people, Joshua 23:3 reminding them that they should remember and don't forget, Deuteronomy 9:7. Reconnecting them to the charge Moses stated before the congregation, Joshua did the same as Moses.

Joshua 24:15, and "if it seems evil unto you to serve the Lord, choose you this day whom you will serve. Whether the god's which your fathers served that were on the other side of the flood, or the god's of the Amorites, in whose land ye dwell, but as for me and my house we shall serve the Lord". Joshua's obedience to completion did put a smile in God's face. Joshua 21:45, "there failed not ought of any good thing which the Lord had spoken unto the house of Israel, all came to pass". Joshua 21:45 said it all regarding God's faithfulness. Joshua died at the age of one hundred and ten years, and he was buried in the border of his inheritance and Joseph's bones which was brought up out of Egypt was buried in Shechem.

Chapter 10
Implementation of the Commandments and Consequences

From the book of Joshua to the book of Esther, it has been Israel's up and down, dancing between the tune of God and tune of the known world. It has been the East wind blowing across releasing judgement and deliverance (Exodus 14:21) for space and time. I will summarize each chapter from Judges to Ruth in that order. The law can never save you. God was trying to let them know this practically, experientially, emotionally and in any way possible, they can understand. Paul tried to explain this in Roman 7 in the Devotional Bible translation, saying that until the law said, "thou shall not covet" then he found himself filled with covetousness of every kind, and he asked why? Answer, the sin within us uses the law itself to produce the very offence the law is intended to prevent. God wanted the Israelites to come to the end of themselves to realize that they needed a Savior to save them, and no two ways about it. The law was only to teach and to point them to the Savior.

The book of Judges. Disobedience escalated after the death of Joshua that the Israelites asked God for a leader. The appointment of Judges didn't help Israel as sin was on high as Judges 21:25 narrated; more must be done. God is already at hand with the answers to their questions and solutions to their problems. Judah(Praise) was to go with them to war with the Canaanites, Judges 3:7. God used Deborah, used Gideon against the Midianites. They built an altar which he called Jehovah-Shalom for their worship and sacrifice. He used Sampson against the Philistines. Remember the story of Sampson and Delilah. It was God calling the Israelites to wake up from sleep, Judges 5:12; This is the set time, "awake, awake Deborah; awake, awake utter a song; arise, Barak and lead thy captivity captive, thou son of Abinoam". God is calling on all sleeping Christians to arise and redeem the lost. You cannot change what you cannot confront.

The book of Ruth. The book of Ruth opened another connection, springing from Naomi's episode involving Ruth a Moabite, Boaz from Bethlehem, who later married Ruth as the hand of God turned things upside down, Ruth 2:12. Boaz said to Ruth, "the Lord recompense thy work and a full reward be given thee of the Lord God of Israel, under whose wings thou art come to trust". Obed is born and the Davidic lineage initiated. Boaz is a type of Christ and you can see how God sorted things out without any damage control. Who says God is not a faithful God, He is.

The most striking issue in the book of Ruth and the lesson one can learn from the book and that is that 'nothing just happens', as easily said by Dr. Creflo Dollar during his TV sermons. God is behind the scene preparing and pulling the strings of connection. When you look at Ruth 1:14-22, you will observe what God is doing. Separation of sheep and goat, the wheat and the tare. Watch the issue Ruth 1:14, who goes and who stays? Naomi pressured them to go, Orpah and Ruth in that even though the compassion was there, time was not on their side, Ruth 1:13. God is moving us systematically, working us up, secretly, silently and supernaturally and nothing can stop it, Isaiah 54:17. Like Jonah who was preparing for Tarshish but God was preparing him for Nineveh. Finally, Naomi had to go with Ruth who proclaimed and declared one of the most striking statements in the Bible found in Ruth 1:16-17. So be it, Naomi agreed, yielded and made course corrections and adjustments emotionally, spiritually to accommodate Ruth, who had vowed that Naomi's God shall be her own God also; Faith, belief and trust at work. Just believe and trust the true God of the true Bible. Ruth convinced and convicted, trusted and obeyed the intuitive knowledge of God in her and the spiritual instinct endowed by God within her.

The book of 1st Samuel. We witnessed the birth of Samuel, Hannah's son who was raised up in the house of Eli the high priest of Israel who failed to discipline his sons properly, 1st Samuel 2:24, "Nay my sons, for it is no good report that I hear. Ye make the Lord's people to transgress". Samuel is called and doom is declared on Eli's family. Defeat and victory of Israel. Israel vehemently demanded a king like other cities ignorantly forgetting the covenant God had with their forefathers Abraham, Isaac and Jacob. All the attitude and behaviors were going against the plans and intention of God.

God instructed Samuel to anoint Saul, 1st Samuel 9:15-21, 10:1-2. Saul did not follow God's instruction so Samuel had to rebuke him for his disobedience, 1st Samuel 13:13. In the story of David and Jonathan, the strength of friendship was exemplified. Here again we can see the power of love stressing the fact that if we can teach the value of love, the strength of love and the power of thinking about the welfare of others, the problem of this world will start to shrink. Saul was later rejected by God and David was chosen to replace Saul because of his continued unwillingness to obey God to completion. 1st Samuel 15: 17-23, Samuel said "when thou was little in thine own sight, wasn't thou not made the head of the tribes of Israel, and the Lord anointed thee King over Israel? For rebellion is as the sin of witchcraft and stubbornness is as iniquity and idolatry". David process to the throne took some time but he continued to validate his love for God. He killed a bear and a lion as a shepherd, killed Goliath, the terrible enemy of Israel. Despite David's lasciviousness, killing and marrying someone's wife, Abigail, wife of Nabal, God still loves him and declared that he was a man after His own heart. It was after the death of Saul that David could breathe in some fresh air around. David knew how to dance God's scriptural tune, the what, the How and why of God. The case of David's readiness to repent as many times as possible shows God's willingness to forgive us as shown in the

New testament, Luke 17:3-4.

The Book of 2nd Samuel. David was mad receiving the news of how Saul and his son were killed. The statement, "how are the mighty fallen, and the weapons of war perished" came to mind, 2nd Samuel 1:27. "The beauty of Israel is slain upon thy high places; how are the mighty fallen" 2 Samuel 1:19. David was anointed King of Israel, 2nd Samuel 5:3. God used David mightily not that David was good but because God is good and has been good and will remain good because He doesn't change. God was pleased with how David was handling issues concerning Him. He knows what pleases God and wastes no time doing that. He brought the Ark of Covenant, back to Jerusalem. David handling of Mephibosheth issue. His relationship with Jonathan. Many people have written a lot about David's life but what I went for was what lessons do I learn from David's life and why should David be a man after God's heart. How do I become a giant killer like David? He easily accepts responsibility for his actions, repent and apologize willingly. He makes up his mind to overcome criticism, often encourages himself and follow God's order all the way through. How do I benefit from these lessons and avoid going through the school of hard knocks, and learn through the experience of these Bible characters like David, Moses, Joseph, their success and failures, their mistakes and corrections? The only thing that can change the society is men and women who are shaped by the love of God and the fear of the Lord as seen in Proverbs 8:13. Read and study the life of David in the second book of Samuel and see what God said, how He said it and why He said it. David was a man after God's 'How'. He knew how to please God and knew how to dance God's tune. Master God's signature tune.

The 1st Kings of the Bible. It's about Elijah. God has now started seriously using people to address the rebellion of the people of Israel. It was clearly noticed that they were doing whatever they liked, full of pride and arrogance as recorded in Judges 21:25. After the death of David, Solomon one of the sons of David was anointed king over Israel. Solomon pleased God and when God asked him what He wants from him, Solomon simply requested for understanding heart to judge his people that he may be able to discern between good and bad. 1st Kings 3:9, God did not only grant him his request, as seen in 1st Kings 3:10-15 but added more than Solomon had expected and requested. This confirms the fact that glorifying and bringing honor to God is what pleases him and immediate compensation was instituted on behalf of Solomon. He lived to build the temple which God denied the father but only started falling off God's track because of strange women. Things became so bad in Israel when Ahab became the king of Israel. Lessons from Solomon the wisest man whose wisdom paraded the known world for a long time but I doubted his wisdom to manage his dealings with the concubines and strange women. Elijah appeared on the scene and armed with a word from God confronted Ahab and Jezebel. This is a man who became bold, courageous, fearless in his approach to revival, called fire from Heaven, destroyed false Baal prophets of Ahab and Jezebel, but succumbed to a hand-written note from Jezebel and decided to run for his dear life. This is a lesson of success and failures exhibiting the power of negative imagination to the fullest. How are the mighty fallen in the Bible? When we forget to remember, or reject to consider what God has said and done, how he has said it and done it, and why he said it and did it, we end up doubting ourselves and blaming others for our failures. One should remember and not forget what is said in Job 14:7-9. Its saying that there is hope for a cut-down tree because through the scent of water, it will bud and bring forth boughs like a plant.

Elijah's story started in 1st Kings 17:1 to 1st Kings 19:1. There were Elijah's success days when he spoke the word of God boldly, confidently, courageously and with love. He did all the killings and from 1st Kings 19:9 he started to doubt himself and God asked him twice what He was doing here? You are where you shouldn't be. He failed twice to correct his wrong answers and his impressions. At prosperity point Elijah became susceptible and vulnerable, 1st King 18:13. Elijah didn't know that the action he was taking will affect other people's lives. God told Elijah to do three things. 1st Kings 19:15-16, 19.

(1) Anoint Hazael to be King over Syria.

(2) Anoint Jehu to be King over Israel and anoint Elisha to be a prophet in thy room.

Elijah did only one thing and for over thirteen years because of Elijah's neglect many people in Israel lost their lives including the life of Naboth, Ist Kings 21:15. Most of the deaths could have been avoided had Elijah done what God had assigned him to do. It took some years before Elisha did what Elijah failed to do. Some writers put it as thirteen years or thereabout. It was in 2nd King 8:13 that Hazael was confirmed king over Syria and in 2nd Kings 9:3 that Jehu was confirmed King over Israel. Elijah saw himself as dead as one of the prophets he had killed and as such got himself out of God's presence and influence. Elijah forgot to remember that the word of God had been his armor but he lowered his shield and completely forgot putting on the whole armor of God.

Despite Elijah's misgivings, God still guided him until the day he departed from Elisha who received a double portion as he requested. This is covered by 2nd Kings 2:9-15. Micaiah's prophecy came within this period of turmoil in Israel and his lifetime witnessed the fall of the Northern Kingdom of Israel. He warned of judgement and of course with double assurance of hopeful expectations of revival. Remember you could be a part of somebody's miracle.

The book of 2nd Kings dealt with Elisha's activities after he has inherited double portion of Elijah's anointing. Even though God left Elijah to finish up that which he didn't do, yet he was still taken up and didn't see death in his lifetime, 2nd Kings 2:10-12. But all that Elijah prophesied happened as and when due. Don't be limited by what you see and don't let circumstances change your identity or dictate who you are in God. Elisha did a lot of miracles like he claimed to have double portion of what Elijah had and did. 2nd Kings was about completion of what Elijah couldn't complete, Hazael and Jehu worked hard under God's direction and did the clean up along with Elisha. All these go on to show us that as long as we are willing to obey, God will always give us answers to our questions and solutions to our problems.

The books of 1st Chronicles and 2nd Chronicles were all written to showcase the issues left behind which weren't dealt with properly. Ezra using all sources available to him, compiled the prophetic recordings of the prophets, portraying the lives of Israel's leaders especially the Kings. The first part dealt with genealogy from Adam to David. The left overs concerning the temple, priesthood, offering and feasts, as the essential elements of her national life was recorded by KJV. The two books are not the same as each has its own purpose. The man who had the courage to believe said five things, the prayer of Jabez.

(1) Bless me indeed

(2) Enlarge my coast,

(3) Let your hand be with me

(4) Keep me from evil

(5) Keep me from grief. Striking issues of Jabez, 1st Chronicles 4:9-10.

Jabez knew he is before God of Israel, He knew he was in covenant with God. He knew the spiritual effects and the spiritual laws that govern the universe. He knows God's capability, availability and willingness to save his people. He knew as a covenant man and a praying man, he can stake a claim if he dares and has the courage to believe God, and God answered him immediately, knowing that he was the seed of Abraham, and that Jabez was aware of what belongs to him and how he can claim it. These are people who knew the How and how to use it. Like Dr. Femi Falana, my advisor says that those who know how to find job will find one but those who know why will be the boss. Jabez knew the 'how' and the 'why' of it all. David's sin in numbering the people is recorded because of its effect on the nation of Israel, but God enabled David to collect the materials for the temple but denied him building it. This closes with Solomon ascending to the throne.

2nd Chronicles. The Chronicles continues with Solomon building the temple. Solomon built the temple per God's specifications and because of his prayers which was not selfish or self-centered, was blessed by God with that temple but didn't stay long to enjoy the temple because of the strange women he allowed into his life. So, after the death of Solomon as covered in 2nd Chronicles 9:21-36 Rehoboam his son took over and Israel was shocked at his wickedness as recorded in 2nd Chronicles 10:1-19 with climax at verse 16. Israel went into division north and south and sin continued to multiply and pile up until Israel out of their own frustration now needed a King against the will and intentions of God. God started using and assigning prophets, prophecies upon prophecies of eminent punishment. Jerusalem was finally destroyed and the inhabitants taken into captivity. The people of Israel were split into north with ten tribes, with Samaria as capital of Israel. South, 2 tribes, Judah with Jerusalem as its capital. We must remember that God has zero tolerance for sin and sin must be punished. In 2nd Chronicles 7:14, God has promised, saying, "if my people which are called by my name, shall humble themselves and pray and seek my face and turn from their wicked ways, then will I hear from heaven and will forgive their sin and will heal their land". So, situation remained critical for both those in captivity and the remnants left in Jerusalem. They were lots and lots of wickedness and rebellion against God's people. So, Chronicles closes with the decree from a pagan king Cyprus King of Persia, permitting the Jews to return from captivity to rebuild the shattered Jerusalem temple. Lessons to be learnt. Even though the children of Israel weren't faithful yet God was faithful because God is good. God's grace is always appropriated through faith and trust in Him.

The Book of Ezra. Ezra and Nehemiah worked hand in hand to repair the broken-down wall of Jerusalem. These last three books, Ezra, Nehemiah and Esther before Job tell of events after the Babylonian captivity. The story of the Kings a matter of nearly five centuries, ended disastrously in 587 BC with the sack of Jerusalem, the fall of the monarchy and the removal to Babylon of all that made Judah a political entity. Their land became desolate. In Ezra's book, he tells of the return of the Jews from Babylonian captivity, the rebuilding of the temple and later coming of Ezra to Jerusalem to instruct the people in the law of God. Nehemiah came to rebuild the broken walls. Remember that Jesus is the rebuilder of the broken walls of our shattered life. Nehemiah gave two-fold lesson of separation from the world and separation unto God. In the books of Ezra and Nehemiah God sends three different ministries.

(1) Zerubbabel came in to lay the foundation of the temple and get it well under way, that is the actual work.

(2) Ezra committed to God and his people, assisted spiritually along with teaching them the law of God which came by Moses.

(3) Nehemiah involved and committed leader came in, to rebuild the wall and bring the people back to holiness and wholeness.

So, Nehemiah succeeded in rebuilding the city wall out-facing his enemies, repopulating Jerusalem and routing within his camp the traitors and enemies of peace. This is covered by Nehemiah 6:10-14. This portion of Nehemiah was what brought about my dissertation summary. Nehemiah 6:11 and I quote, "and I said should such a man as I flee? And defile the holy place of God?" Nehemiah knew what God wanted him to do, how he wanted him to do it, and why he wanted him to do it. And who is that being, to deceive me to go into the temple of God to save my life? I will not go in. Nehemiah knew that he has a God that can defend and protect him in his assignment from his known and unknown enemies. So, he decreed and declared as such in Nehemiah 6:14 and I quote, "My God think you upon Tobiah and Sanballat per their works and on the prophetess Noadiah and the rest of the prophets could have put me in fear". I have applied Nehemiah's verse of the scripture and saw that God will always protect his words like it's said in scriptures 2nd Chronicle 16:9a, "for the eyes of the Lord run to and fro throughout the whole earth to shew himself strong in the behalf of them whose heart is perfect towards Him".

This also is written in Psalms 32:8, "I will instruct thee and teach thee in the way which thou shall go. I will guide thee with mine eye". I applied Nehemiah 5:19, NIV, which says, "remember me with favor, oh my God for all I have done for these people". I was one day travelling home to see my people and after we were set to go, my 2nd son and myself stood behind my front door and I decreed and declared Nehemiah's statement of chapter 5:19 and we left for the airport. Right in the airport, I was the first person to be checked in even though we were in line and I wasn't originally the first in line. An airport staff just came from nowhere and beckoned me to come up front to be checked in. My son looked at me and I looked at him and there I went and was checked in. It took another hour before the actual checking-in started. So, I went in and relaxed, reading my books and occasionally making phone calls before our departure.

I thanked God for his favor which continue to follow all through my journey to and from USA. God is always faithful to those who believe and trust Him. But you must be sure you have done something recognizable or tangible for your people to justify that claim.

The Book of Esther. Even though God is not mentioned once by name, yet no book of Bible shows more wonderfully the providential care of God for His people and the indestructibility of the Jewish race. This shows the faithfulness of God. Esther must look at her life based on her calling and not based on her beauty or intellect or position. You can't change what you can't confront. You must view life through the grid of God's intentions. Life is not what you expect but what you permit. The Jews were at the point of being annihilated and their existence was in jeopardy. Esther and Mordecai had to fish out a plan to protect themselves and the Jewish people. After Esther and Mordecai met, Mordecai released a profound declaration of the highest order in Esther 4:14 to Esther and I quote; "For if thou altogether holdest thy peace at this time, then shall their enlargement and deliverance arise to the Jews from another place, but thou and thy fathers house shall be destroyed. And who knoweth whether thou art come to the kingdom for such a time as this". Esther proclaimed a three day fast for her people and made a powerful, tearful producing statement written down in Esther 4:16 and I quote in part the conclusion after her order. "I Esther will go unto the king which is not according to the Law, and if I perish I perish". So, Mordecai went his way and did per all that Esther had commanded him. God's providential protection assured. God will always save His people. There are always scriptural promised answers and solutions afloat, Proverbs 26:2, curse causeless shall not come. About Haman's plot against the Jews, I quote Macbeth,

Williams Shakespeare's book, "for false face must hide what the false heart doth knew" (Shakespeare 1977, 18). Haman of Esther chapter 7, paid highly for this hatred of the Jews. The Bible made it clear, that we shouldn't let our differences mar the togetherness we have in God. This is always a sign of spiritual freedom and maturity. Remember that there are things to believe and things to do.

The book of Job is thought to be one of the oldest portions of the word of God. Along with Psalms, Proverbs, Ecclesiastes, the Song of Solomon and Lamentations are recognized as the language of the heart and by nature experiential. Job and Lessons from it. Remember it's still the what, the How, and Why of God. God's signature tune. Job didn't know what was happening, didn't understand How it started and had no knowledge why it started. In the first place, the question posed is a universal one, "why do the righteous suffer"? God did answer the question through the concrete experience of a righteous man. Many who suffer for years overlook the fact that God called Job a perfect and upright man, Job 1:1,8, Job 2:3. For now we must remember that Satan has no access to God in Heaven. When Jesus took His blood back, He cleansed heaven of the presence of Satan. But before then, Satan did have access. In the Old Testament and the millennial reign people were commanded to appear for accountability before God, Job 1:6. Satan's evil mind is an open book to God. God's question to Satan concerning Job revealed Satan's intentions but believed that his lack of success in his evil intentions was because of God's divine hedging on Job, Job 1:10. Realistically, Job didn't sin with his mouth, but did let down the hedge and this allowed Satan to attack him, Job 1:5,10. Job gave a pious and religious answer Job 1:20-22 which many religious preachers have taken out of context.

What Job 1:20-22 said, is said by Job and not by God. It is true that God gives but it is Satan who takes away. Job's reaction would have been different if he had been aware of Heaven's counsel before his trials began. Job's trials originated in heaven and finished in enrichment and blessing. His wife and his four friends theorized from incomplete knowledge, they knew nothing about the coming compensation. There is an explanation for everything that happens to us. God is sovereignly in charge but gave us power and authority over the control of the earth. However, Job acknowledged that the mistake of his friends is in their thinking and assuming that all suffering is because of personal sin was in itself wrong. Job stated that nothing can change God's mind, Job 23:13-17 and though troubled and perplexed and constantly asking why? his faith was sublime and real, Job 19:25. Jobs reply to God solves the problem of suffering Job 42:1-6.

The greatest lesson of Job to me is found in Job 14:7-9 where it said in part, "for there is hope of a tree, if it be cut down, that it will sprout again and that the tender branch thereof will not cease, yet through the scent of water, It will bud and bring forth boughs like a plant". In conclusion Job was a good man who recognized and accepted his need of the righteousness of God, Romans 7:18, 24, 25. Job was caught in the middle between God and Satan as the sailors were caught in between God and Jonah.

The next series are the Psalms, the Proverbs and Ecclesiastes. Ray C. Stedman's Adventuring through Bible Series, did a good job in calling Psalms songs of a sincere heart, the book of human emotions. He called Proverbs, what life is all about and Ecclesiastes, the Inspired Book of Error. In his analysis, he shows that the Psalms were book of ancient Israel. The deepest insight that you can gain into the heart of the Psalms is to understand that these songs of faith fully and beautifully reveal the work and the person of Jesus Christ. Another writer Garnett Reid in his survey of Old Testament, wrote that "the purpose of these proverbs is to give the reader a profile of God's wisdom, knowledge, understanding, providence and discretion.

"Anyone who wants these qualities to characterize his or her life will want to drink deeply from this book" (Reid 2014, 36). What can I say about Ray Stedman's reference to Proverbs in his book, Adventuring through Psalms, Proverbs and Ecclesiastes, than to concur with him that "in order to successfully navigate the swirling current of our daily existence with all of its temptations, deceptions, and risky choices, we need wisdom - the timeless, dependable, true wisdom of God" (Stedman 1997, 18). All these people are writing from the true Bible telling us what God has said and done, how He said it or how He did what He said and why He said and did what He said. I thank them for their contributions. From Psalms 1 to Psalms 150, my favorite being Psalms 103:2, which says, "praise the Lord O my soul and forget not all his benefits". Know your purpose and be focused.

The questions are there and the answers are there, the problems are out there and the solutions are out there. Theology is all about what God said, how what God said became what He intended, Genesis 1:3, and God said let there be light and there was light. How God said it, and it turns to be how God wanted it, why God said it and it became why God intended it to be. I'm in agreement, with Pastor Lawson Perdue statement that "God's word created the heavens and the earth. What he speaks creates and changes reality to confirm to his word. When he calls something that is not as though it was, the Word He spoke releases power to change the situation" (Perdue 2014, 17). He quoted Psalms 33:6,9 NIV and then Romans 4:17b. From all this, we can see that God's power is voice activated as seen in Genesis 3, that is God said series of the Bible. What God speaks is not only true but becomes Truth.

Song of Solomon. In 1st King 4:32, we are told that Solomon wrote 1005 songs and is taken as the best among equals. This is the love story that glorifies pure, natural affection and points to the simplicity and sanctity of marriage. The Jewish people assume the work as surely symbolic or typical of Yahweh's love for Israel while Christians take it as Christ's love for the church. Of the five books called the rolls, read from ancient times the Song of Solomon is read in the synagogue annually at the Passover, the first great feast of the Jews/Hebrew. The bridegroom calls the bride "my Love" and the bride refers to him as "my beloved". The purpose and significance of love has been taught, preached and that's why Ray. C. Stedman reminded us in his book 'Lessons from Leviticus' that God particularly regulated for the people of Israel "two areas of life, their behavior towards blood and their behavior towards sex", page 208. The book of Lamentation written by Jeremiah has been regarded as the diary of Jeremiah weeping over the coming destruction of Jerusalem. The sorrow of Jeremiah and that of God is seen throughout the book of Lamentation. This shows how faithful God is and how delighted He is when people have the courage to trust Him enough to voice and place their concerns and sorrows in his hand. By calling to God for our problems and our inability to solve them means our dependence on Him, our faith on Him, our leaning on Him.

I will be dealing with all the prophets together from Isaiah to Malachi with small emphasis on some of them. As we go through this portion of scripture, we keep in mind that these prophets were writing about Israel's sin and were warning them that if they did not change and repent, God would surely punish them. The Bible as many writers have written is regarded as our moral and spiritual reality check as 1st Timothy 3:16 rightly pointed out. We don't need to look at the negatives, but look at God reluctance to dispense judgment as seen in 2nd Peter 3:9. Look for his overwhelming compassion and most of all, look for His love for His people. God's original intention was that all of Israel were to be priests unto Him, but the people vehemently did not want that. It is broken fellowship that causes most of the problems. When we miss the mark and are sorry, God is there to pick us up. As repentance goes with fellowship, David could be cited as the most repentant Old Testament candidate and had his benefit as the man after God's heart. God was responsible for calling upon the prophets and assigning them responsibilities per need and location taking into consideration the social, spiritual need of each audience. Each prophet was armed with message from God to be delivered as and when due. The prophets were regarded as official spokesman for God. The prophets represent God before men while the priest represents men before God. The prophetic office came into prominence after the division of the kingdom as Israel and Judah declined morally and spiritually in all aspects of life. From all available records, God used whoever He deems useful to fulfill his plans and purposes.

Some of these prophets are known to have not written any biblical books and such non-writing prophets include, Nathan, Elijah, Elisha and some others we don't even know. When we think of Bible prophecy, individuals like Isaiah, Daniel, Jeremiah, Ezekiel do come to mind not merely because of their contribution but because of the length of time. They are regarded as the major prophets and the rest regarded as minor prophets. Prophecy may concern the past the present or as we notice mostly the future. All these activities go to buttress the fact that God made promised answers to our questions available and every problem has its scriptural promised solutions. God is now using humans to let his creation know and be aware of God's unlimited power to make sure that none of His words fall to the ground unfulfilled, Isaiah 55:11. The promise is for unlimited resources to do the work of God.

The use of special delegates, the prophets and even seers came to be, when all means of communication seemed to be failing regarding the in balance of how man do behave and how they ought to behave, coupled with the deep-rooted rebellion among the people of God. This is what Hank Kunneman had to say; "in the Bible, God always had a prophetic voice that carries the secrets of the Lord to Kings and leaders of nations. Still today, as Revelation 4:1 indicates, doors are being opened in heaven to receive throne-room secrets, and at the same time, doors are opening in the earth for us to share these secrets which show the heart and will of God for all people, even leaders of nations" (Kunneman 2009, 2). Kunneman said further that "it is not uncommon for God to place a spokesman who has heavenly secrets in his or her mouth to minister to leaders and that prophetic words should be a key element affecting nations in a positive way" (Kunneman 2009, 2). It is still the war of words, still the unanswered question of 'How' that has been left unattended to. It is time to act and react.

It is still what the Almighty God is saying, How He has been saying it and why He has been saying it. Remember that these prophets are being armed with the word of God from the throne-room. In 1st King 17, Elijah could speak to Ahab because he was armed with the word of God so also other prophets like Isaiah, Jeremiah, Ezekiel and Daniel to mention but a few, had to function without fear or favor because of the knowledge of throne-room secrets. They have now been delegated and authorized to represent God on earth.

God has already demonstrated His capability, His availability and His willingness as to what He has confirmed and established, spiritually, physically and emotionally. The prophecies were pointing out to the incoming Messiah who will deliver us from the sin that did separate us from God. We can see the power of willingness as expressed in Isaiah 1:19; "If ye be willing and obedient Ye shall eat the good of the land. It didn't say if you are obedient you will eat the good of the land". The Bible is saying that If we obey rightly and obey to completion, there would be so much to eat even in our old age. In marriage, people often say I do but don't. What you know and believe is governed by this word 'if'. For Isaiah, obedience is validated by one's willingness, like the spiritual instinct that differentiated the one leper out of the 10 lepers that Jesus healed, only one was healed and made whole. This was what John Bevere mentioned in his book, The Undercover which illustrates one's willingness to obey an authority. What He is saying in effect is to know whether you will be willing under any condition to obey and consider only God's words. People have agreed yet disagreed at the same time and obeyed to do something and yet failed completely to do it. They don't even trust the obeying issue. If you are willing, it means you are committed to do it come rain come shine. I am involved and committed to obey the authority that is the honor. The right to command and be obeyed. These are the highlights of some of God's signature tune, the Whats, Hows, and Whys of the Bible. God made it clear that He will do nothing without first revealing his intentions to his prophets, making it clear what is of Him, and How it should be done and why it should be done as purposed, Isaiah 42:9, and Amos 3:7.

In Isaiah God started the preaching of the gospel. Telling them what to do, teaching them how to say it and do it and why it should be done that way. A close look at some chapters of Isaiah will bring home to us lots and lots of what God had said and done, How He said it and did it and the why. Isaiah is saying it as instructed in Isaiah 45:2,3,11, Isaiah 46:9-10, Isaiah 53:10, Isaiah 55:8,11, Isaiah 61:1, Isaiah 65:21,24. Isaiah 54:14, 17, concluded it all by saying that in righteousness shall thou be established in part verse 14 and then that no weapon formed against you shall prosper in part verse 17. He is prophesying the future. Jeremiahs 29:11 assured us of God's intentions, his purpose and plans for us as his creation. In Jeremiah 35:1-19, Jabez removed himself from the negative statistics to positive statistics because he knew He was a covenant candidate. In Ezekiel, God assuring us that we have the power to use his words to prophesy. Ezekiel 37:1-13 deals with the issue of dry bones, what to say, how to say it and why of the prophecy.

Daniel. In Daniel 9:25-26 the angel Gabriel revealed to Daniel the timetable for the Messianic age, How He divinely showed him the Messianic calculations. Who says that calculations are not important?

Martin R. DeHaan said that "when calculations are carefully handled, they can be an important indicator to resolve controversial issues. We can't afford to ignore the numbers that have the potential to resolve such disputes" (DeHaan II 2007, 1). In Daniel like in Jabez, God showed Israel for all generations and us today because we are covenant man, that a praying person can stake a claim (like Jabez and Daniel did) if he dares and has the courage and fortitude to believe God completely. They know the How and enforced the Law of How just like a police man enforcing the law of the land.

In Hosea, God shows Israel the state of things by Hosea's marriage to a harlot named Gomer. Israel was running outside the will of God and God had to send prophets to start afresh warning them.

(1) In Joel 2:13 a call for repentance or suffer the consequences.

(2) Amos 3:7 message to his prophets.

(3) Jonah 2:8, use Jonah's rebellion to address Nineveh's rebellion. Jonah was the most qualified to do this job because He was just entering from where he came from.

(4) Micah 7:18 God's pardon and love, Believe and trust.

(5) Obadiah (east wind), judgement and deliverance.

(6) Nahum 1:3 perseverance.

(7) Habakkuk 2:4, the just shall live by faith.

(8) Zephaniah, call to repentance 2:1-3, for you to hold your peace

and the power of holding onto your peace.

(9) Haggai, consider your ways, examine your ways.

(10) Zechariah 4:6 not by power nor by might but by my spirit saith the Lord of hosts.

(11) Malachi, the sin of priesthood 1:6, tithing and offering by law.

There is a mix up here as some preachers use the requirements of the law in Old Testament against the requirement of Grace in New Testament. Don't mix Grace and law. Mixing them will be like pouring new wine into old wine bottle which the scripture doesn't advice, Mark 2:21-22.

All that are been said are all pointing to the coming of the Messiah. What did God say about His coming? How is He going to come and why is He coming? All these will be dealt with in the New Testament showing us that the Bible is all about what God said and did. How He said and did it and why He did it. All our Questions and all our problems are scripturally being handled with promised answers to our questions and promised solutions to our problems. The new requirement is just to believe and receive. Our emphasis is the How's of God. In Isaiah 58:8-11 God is showing us the How as revealed to Isaiah the prophet. In Daniel 5:23, Daniel is telling us what to drop off and what we must consider in other to position ourselves for God's promises to come to pass. Reconsider your ways and adjust if need be. Let the practicing Christians be on the offensive and enforce the kingdom agenda and develop the kingdom mindset and stop being on the defensive. Our people normally say don't sit on the fence, joint the civil defense, in protecting your town or country during civil disturbances. This takes the dissertation to part three, the preparation and arrival of the Messiah. It's all about the what, the How and Why of the Bible. Be prepared and stay prepared. "Remember that often the problem has been that the rights and privileges receive more acknowledgement of members than the responsibilities and relationship" (Tidwell 1985, 48). Part 3 and 4 will address this issue as the Messiah arrives as the son of man and son of God. It must be noted that the Israelites were rebellious and stubborn in their dealings with God during their journey to the promised land and had to pay dearly for it. They tempted God as shown in Psalms 78:41 and displayed arrogance in not waiting for God's counsel nor demonstrated any appreciation or gratitude during that travel. God despite all these misgivings, supplied them with whatever they needed and desired, but did send leanness into their soul as recorded in Psalms 106:13-15.

PART THREE

Christs Arrival: Before Going to the Cross

Chapter 11

The Connection – John the Baptist's Involvement

Parts 1 and 2 of my dissertation, dealt with the events of what happened before and after Moses arrival and departure, parallels what I am about to write on Parts 3 and 4 of my dissertation concerning what happened and was happening before Jesus' arrival and departure. The changes from Old Testament requirements to New testament requirements under the new covenant and dispensation, are recorded. God's capability, God's availability and God's willingness assured us that all these scriptural promised answers and solutions are based on what God said and did, How and Why He said and did them from the foundation of the earth. "The emphasis in Christian teaching is on the person of Christ. He is the WHAT, He is the HOW and He is the WHY" (Lebar 1995, 155). This book revealed a lot to me during my post-graduate courses in Theology. Our dean Dr. Falana who introduced this book to us said that the book written so many years ago is still relevant today as it was twenty, thirty years ago when it was first written, page 155. Ray C Stedman made a similar comment in his book, Adventuring through Romans, 1st and 2nd Corinthians, saying, "cultures change and circumstances change, but people, their challenges, and their essential needs are the same today as they were then, making Romans and 1st and 2nd Corinthians as practical and relevant today, as they were nearly 2000 years ago" (Stedman 1997, 5). Jesus has now arrived to put us through the How series, which He illustrated so vividly in John's gospel, as we will see later, John chapters 14-16. He has arrived to destroy the works of the devil 1st John 3:8.

Dr. J. Sidlow Baxter stated, "the period between Malachi and Mathew covers some 400 years, if we accept the usual date assigned to Malachi. This 400-year interval has been called the dark period of Israel's history in pre-Christian times because through it there was neither prophet nor inspired writers. We may say that Jewish history during those four centuries between the testaments runs in six periods; the Persian, the Greek, the Egyptian, the Syrian, the Maccabean and the Romans" (Baxter 1996, 11,13).

The expectations of Israel were high and knowing that God goes by patterns and processes, kept them confused. We must know the purpose and the significance of what is being expected, what was discussed and examined and what was decided and decreed. The New Testament is the word of God written under the inspiration of the Holy Spirit as stated in 2nd Timothy 3:16. The process started with John the Baptist being the fore-runner who was testifying to Christ's coming. The Lamb of God who has come to lay aside the penalty of sin, the practice of sin and the presence of sin. Jesus has come prepared to both fulfill and complete the Old Testament. This is what the prophets have been prophesying expecting (1st Peter 1:10,12) and the angels warming up, for John the Baptist to open the door. The first gospels written centered on Jesus message and the significance and meaning of His life, death and resurrection. As John 1:17 said, "the law was given by Moses but grace and truth came by Jesus Christ". It then means that the practicing believers should make this teaching of Christ the center of their life and conduct, and everyone else given a chance, an opportunity to respond to this grace and truth. It is a question of responding positively or negatively to the gospel of Christ. Tim Lahaye said that "before the human race was created in the garden of Eden there was a conflict between God and His most powerful angel, Satan (Lucifer). For some reason Satan thought he was equal with God. Even today he evidently thinks he could wrest control of this universe from God himself. The Bible shows that from the creation of humankind to the present there has been endless conflict for the will and soul of people to see if they would use that free will to obey God or Satan" (Lahaye 1999, 196-197). Like David Roper wrote in his book, "you need to remember that even if power has been wrested from your hands, there are other hands at work. Behind every human act, lies the action of one whose will is indomitable and whose power is supreme" (Roper 2008, 134).

This act of disobedience resulted in pushing Satan (Lucifer) out of heaven together with angels loyal to him, Isaiah 14:12-16. Jesus arrived here in the flesh, 100% human and 100% God, this is termed Hypostatic union, as referred to by many writers, one of them being Kevin J Conner, in his book The Foundations of Christian Doctrine. Christ Jesus was one person, having in Himself the union of two natures; the nature of God and the nature of man. This is how He was able to handle Mathew 5:17. Thus constituting Him the God-Man. Now we are moving naturally from the need for help to the promises of God, from law and order of Moses to the grace and truth of Christ. David Roper says that "beyond the bad news of failure, is the good news of grace - the stupendous free gift of God; Grace also means that God has given us the resources to make a new beginning" (Roper 2008, 38). It's time to put off the old requirement of the law and put on the new requirement of Grace and Truth. To understand the New Testament which is old covenant revealed, we must understand the Old Testament which is the New Covenant concealed. Old Testament; It is the Torah or the Law which is the center of the all in all. New Testament; It is all about Jesus Christ, who is the center of the universe, the All in All, the Alpha and Omega. The struggles and conflicts of bringing down cultural legacies of the Roman empire, the scattered Jewish communities and the many religious cultures created a challenging context for the preaching of the gospel of Jesus Christ as the 'Study Bible commentary of KJV' narrated. The introduction to the 'Study Bible KJV' by Thomas Nelson emphasized that the New

Testament "is the best attested ancient document in the world. The necessity of proclaiming God's New Covenant to all people demands that they can read the life-changing provisions of this arrangement in their own language", page 1400. Here again it is what Jesus said and did, how and why he said and did it all. He gathered his people and started preparing them for the ministry and was always mindful of where he came from and where he was going.

All the four gospels narrated the life of Christ, his teaching, the signs and wonders and all they needed to know and understand about the Trinity. The diversity of the congregation made it difficult, coupled with the engrafted law mindset of the religious group added salt to injury. So, the four gospels were written based on the ministry of Jesus Christ before going to the cross. It was introductory class before the proper exposure. The basic purpose of the Gospels is to present the gospel message, the good news of the Redeemer-Savior of the World. It was on the first things first, calculations from the first principle as I call it, expressing the wisdom of God, the knowledge of God and the understanding of God. Moving from sin consciousness to Christ consciousness, definition of things or words, and reasonings should go through the Bible. We have now moved from what God said to what Christ said.

The four Gospel by Matthew, Mark, Luke and John presented four portraits of Christ, each applying the concept of hermeneutics as outlined by Henry A. Virkler and Karelynne Gerber Ayayo in their 2nd edition of Hermeneutics. The different people they were writing to needed an explanation, involving the knowledge and application of Hermeneutics. To teach Hermeneutics with the required understanding will require stressing the importance of cultural gaps, the historical gaps, the philosophical gap and the linguistic gap. Per Henry A. Virkler, for "a statement to be considered accurate when it meets the level of precision intended by the writer and expected by his audience, that is when understood within the context of their intended purpose. Thus, the affirmation that God is accurate and truthful in all what he says in Scripture should be understood within the context of the level of precision that he intended to communicate" (Virkler and Ayayo 1981, 39). Jesus whose total years from birth to finish was thirty-three years, used three years to cover and fulfill his mission on earth. He knew where he was going and He remembered what should be remembered and like the New Living Translation Study bible 2nd ed. put it, "in the 400 years between the last of Old testament books and the beginning of New testament history, Jewish thinking underwent radical changes under the extended influences of Persian rule, Greek language and philosophy and renewed nationalism", page 1554. These layers upon layer of confusion, frustration, deceits, miss-directions, fear, unbelief and doubts must be dealt with. The New Testament which completes God's revelation was written based on what Jesus had come to restore. As Myer Pearlman put it, "by virtue of His assuming our nature and dying for our sins, Jesus is a mediator between God and man, 1st Timothy 2:5. He is both the Mediator and an Intercessor. Intercessor is an important ministry of the ascended Christ, Roman's 8:34. He died for us. He rose for us. He ascended for us and makes intercession for us. Christ priesthood is eternal; therefore, His intercession is permanent" (Pearlman 2007, 179). Remember that Jesus was born without the seed of sin.

Explanation to the four gospels. There were four representative classes of people during the apostolic period, the Jews, the Romans, the Greeks and the body taken from all three classes, the Church. Each one of the gospel writers wrote for these respective classes, each with a different emphasis according to their character, need and ideals. The need for hermeneutic knowledge was really required for them to understand clearly what God is saying, what Jesus has come to do, How God has done it and why Christ is here to fulfill the Old testament requirements which no other person can do in other to redeem us. Our questions, problems, their answers and solutions are found in this man the Messiah, Colossians 1:19.

(1) So, Matthew, writing for the Jews, presents Jesus as Messiah, King and Humanity.

(2) Mark, writing to the Romans, a people whose ideals was power and service, presents Jesus as the Mighty Conqueror and servant.

(3) Luke, writing to a cultural people, the Greeks presents Jesus as the ideal, perfect man, the son of man.

(4) John, having in mind the needs of Christians of all nations, presents the deeper truths of the Gospel, the deity of Jesus Christ and the Holy Spirit. Jesus is represented as the Son of God. The entire Gospel is for all men.

(a) One has got to acknowledge the fact that one gospel was not going to sufficiently present the many sides of Christ.

(b) Each writer views Jesus from a different aspect, which explains their omissions, additions, seeming contradictions and lack chronological order.

(c) The gospel writers did not attempt a biography of Jesus Christ, they selected the incidents and discourses which would emphasize their message.

The Bible doesn't contradict itself, but interprets itself, complement itself. If we can look at what 2nd Timothy 2:15 is saying and apply it in our interpretation, we will realize the truth of the gospel. It says and I quote from the Amplified bible, comparative study bible, "study and be eager and do your utmost to present yourself to God, approved (tested by trial), a workman who has no cause to be ashamed, correctly analyzing and accurately dividing, rightly handling and skillfully teaching the word of truth". Example, Matthew 8:28-34 and Mark 5:1-20. (a) Matthew presents the factual story, two men. (b) Mark tells the same story, but from the aspect of the one man who came to Jesus and desired to follow him. (c) Mark tells the story of the man who was redeemed. (d) Matthew is telling the total story. It is now a question of studying the Bible to be wise, believe it to be saved, and practice it to be holy. Real love puts action into good intentions.

The first three writers, Matthew, Mark and Luke are referred to as Synoptic Gospels. Synoptic Greek = able to be seen together, viewed together; Syn = with, together; Optanomai = to see. These first three Gospels gave an account of the same events in Jesus' life. The Gospel of John was written on an entirely different plan and was written many years after the other three. There are some differences between the synoptic Gospels and the Gospel of John.

(1) The Synoptic contain an evangelistic message for unspiritual men. John contains a spiritual message of Christians.

(2) The Synoptic concern Jesus Galilean ministry. John concerns Jesus Judean ministry.

(3) The synoptic display Jesus more public life. In John, we are shown His private life.

(4) In Synoptic, we are impressed with humanity of Jesus. In John, we are impressed with His deity, divine.

There are three major truths of importance why we should study the New Testament.

(1) To realize that Jesus came to bear our sins and take the responsibility upon himself of our sin nature. John 12:32, here it is saying that when He is lifted from the earth, He will draw

all judgement unto Himself.

(2) To understand that we are restored to full fellowship and intimacy with the father and enjoy the same relationship with the Father that the Lord Jesus Christ Himself has.

(3) To know and be aware that Jesus overthrew the devil in our place, that we may be free from the Devil's family and that we know now that we can dominate the devil. Moving from old mindset to new mindset, with the engrafted word of God, James 1:21. Our knowledge of what God has said and done, how and why He said and did them, His wishes, gives us hope and assurance that everything God has said, every pronouncement He has made, every statement he uttered is a promise, based on His good intentions for His created order and reflects His immutable character.

This goes with my dissertation that God demonstrates His divine love for His creation and by sending His son to come and reconcile, restore, and restructure mankind through sacrifice which goes beyond any imagination. By this God wants us to know and remember that there is a biblically promised solution and answer to every encounter in life. Our understanding of the 'What', the 'How' and the 'Why' of the Bible which I have called the Signature tune of God will reveal to us who we are in Him. It represents the Trinity, the God of what. What He has said and done. Jesus the How, Jesus paid the price to appease God's wrath and anger and showed us how God did what He said. How we can now live a life of abundance, John 10:10. The Holy Spirit came to be our comforter and to bring us up to God's standard by guiding us, reminding us of why God wants us to do things using His own methods as Jesus has demonstrated. Jesus has confirmed and established this accordingly. Everything about Christianity is based on this signature tune of God, (the What, the How and the

Why). All issues can now be settled through discovering all about God's signature tune. The Almighty Father has made every scriptural promise available to us the believers with the intent to fulfill. Let us belong to the whosoever and whatsoever, based on the signature tune of God. Jesus' disciples were always asking how? John 14:5. How can we know the way? Thomas asked. Jesus replied, that it was in knowing Him that you know that way and not only knowing the way, but also knowing the truth and the life. That is what brought about the song of Graham Kendrick, Knowing You Jesus.

Remember, it all starts with knowing the word of God, trusting Him and submitting to His authority. That's what this dissertation is all about. We must let people know that there is a God to be believed, the God that created the universe. Everyone should be given a chance to hear this good news of Jesus Christ then make a choice to believe or reject. You have no earthly reason not to believe, Romans 1:18-21. The choice is yours but the choice of consequences is not yours because you reap what you sow. Jesus used the How question of Thomas to answer Phillips question and kicked off the How series as we go on in this series. For Christians, the starting point is our willingness to receive the word of God, accept it and like Ephesians 1:6 noted that believers receive this gift of faith of Christ Jesus and His finished work on the cross. A.W Tozer wrote that "when you bring your life into line with your faith, you are a believer" (Tozer 2010, 52). What remains is learning How to use the How of God correctly and appropriately.

I agree with the comments made by Dick Iverson and Bill Scheidler that "everything that begins in Genesis, ends up in the book of Revelation, noting that Genesis is the seed-plot of the Bible. In Genesis, we are told how man lost the image of God when he fell into sin and did corrupt his way. Revelation is the ultimate which tell us the final state of all things. We also see the work of redemption completed" (Iverson and Scheidler 1976, 51). We must remember as I do, that God's first touch was in creation and His second touch was in redemption. Dick Iverson continued, we see man restored to the Tree of Life. Between Genesis 3:24 and Revelation 21:3-5, we see the panorama of restoration in its fullest sense. This confirms that for every question we have, there is scriptural promised answer and for every problem that do confront us there is a scriptural promised solution. In conclusion, Dick Iverson stated and I quote; "Restoration was the theme of the old testament prophets. The prophets were divinely inspired to warn God's people of their backsliding ways and idolatry. By proclaiming God's message, the prophet endeavored to awaken the conscience of the people and to restore them to righteousness and divine fellowship Amos 5:14" (Iverson and Scheidler 1976, 51).

In my own contribution here, I would personally say that I was compelled after my mother's death to acknowledge the existence of God. This was how I viewed the How of the Bible in surviving the problem of being from a polygamous family. All these I learnt during my Sunday school days in an elementary school starting with why God said and did what He said and How. So, our evangelism should start with the why of the Bible. Why did Jesus have to come? All the Whys, He was ready to answer and show us the How based on what God had said and did. As our evangelism must start with the Why of it and the reason for it must go through the Bible to make that reason reasonable. This is how the question raised by C.S. Lewis in his book Mere Christianity can be sorted out.

Like C.S Lewis said, "you find out more about God from the Moral Law than from the Universe in general" (Lewis 1980, 29). On page 9,17,18, he vividly showed and demonstrated the use of 'How' in his illustration of moral issues, "telling us what the Law of Human nature means. The law of Human nature, (which we also call the moral law or rule of decent behavior) tells you what human being ought to do and not do. In order words, when you are dealing with humans, something else comes in above and beyond the facts. You have the facts (how men do behave) and you have something else (how they ought to behave)" (Lewis 1980, 9, 17-18). To help in understanding this issue, I would beg your indulgence to call in Prof M.J. Erickson's explanation that "rendering something certain and rendering it necessary, and distinguishing this, is the key to unlocking the problem" (Erickson 1998, 383). Psalm 11:3 says, "if the foundation is broken, what will the righteous do". It doesn't say what will a politician do or what will a professional do. The responsibility of fixing whatsoever is broken lies with the practicing Christians in the body of Christ and the moral laws is the foundation of Christianity. And like Ravi Zacharias said in James Robison's program while addressing Christian leaders recently in Texas USA, he said that Rich Moral soil is the only thing that can hold the tree and sustain the foundation; showing that moral stability is expected to be found in all Christians. This issue I will continue to explain, as we go into the 'Hows', as Christ unfolds it to our comprehension.

Bill Crowder also wrote that, "we do not learn character in times of ease and prosperity but in times of difficulty. The greatest lessons of life are often the product of our most serious heartaches", (Crowder 1998, 2). In the world, there're more questions and more problems than answers and solutions because as C.S. Lewis stated, "we are living in a part of the universe occupied by the rebel" (Lewis 1980, 45). Paul also in his letter to the Philippians Phil 2:15, wrote this as an example of the likely questions and problems of the human race. The questions and problems are there but there are scriptural promised answers and solutions to those who believe and are willing to apply or practice the already promised answers and promised scriptural solutions. Psalms 145:13 tells us that the Lord is trustworthy in all His promises and he is loyal to all he has made, Max Lucado, Devotional Bible, Hebrews

10:23, 2nd Corinthians 1:20 are all evidence of God's capability, availability and willingness.

There is a proof of the spirit of power, 1st Cor 2:4, God became man that we might become God. Matthew presents Jesus as the promised Messiah who would come and set free not only Israel, but the whole world. The only way man could be restored was only by God, since we have lost the knowledge of God and the image of God in which we were made. Mary was not the Mother of God, she was the Mother of Jesus, The man. God had no mother or father, He existed eternally. In naming of Jesus Christ, we find (a) His Humanity, Jesus, Son of Man. (b) His deity, Christ the Son of God. (c) Incarnate, and His birth marks a dividing part of human history.

Many writers have written a lot about the birth of Christ, the incarnate word of God, stressing the purpose and the significance of the incarnation. Here again I owe my extra knowledge on these topics from the recommended books of the Newburgh Theological Seminary, like The Pursuit of God by A.W. Tozer, The Spirit of Early Christian Thought by Robert Wilken, Mere Christianity by C.S. Lewis, and Christian Theology by Millard Erickson, a distinguished professor of Theology.

Here we go from before Christ to the year of the Lord, a time prepared and ordained by God. Jesus' birth in Bethlehem and life in Nazareth was not by chance. He came when all the preparations had been made, Galatians 4:4. Even Satan, the Spoiler, the Accuser had a hand in Christ's arrival as stated in 2nd Thessalonians 2:9, in keeping with fulfilling the last two verses of Malachi 4:5-6, the world conditions were ready for God's revelation, social, economic, moral religion and all other factors had come together to provide the proper setting for the manifestation of the son of God. The known world had been unified under Caesar and was under Roman domination.

All frontiers between all the countries were now open. There were great roads and good means of travel. There was no language barrier, because all the people knew Greek after Alexander the Great had made it the official language.

My dissertation has been on the 'Hows' and the 'Whys' of the Bible. Many Biblical writers have contributed to clear the questions, the doubts and fears of believing this aspect of the Bible. The book on Documents of the Christian Church edited by Henry Bettensen and Chris Mauder did a good job. Like I stated earlier, this book touching on the defense of the gospel, dealt with atonement and then touched on Salvation by restoration and Salvation by revelation showing us How God made it through redemption and Salvation.

Chapter 12
Matthew's Account

Many embrace Salvation without acknowledging redemption. I will quote Athanasius write up precisely in each of the Salvation by restoration and Salvation by revelation.

(a) In page 36, VI, Salvation by restoration says, "it was reasonable that the Word who is above all, in offering his own temple and bodily instrument as a substitute-life for all, fulfilled the liability in his death, and thus the incorruptible son of God, being associated with all mankind by likeness to them, naturally clothed all with incorruption in the promise concerning the resurrection" (Bettensen and Maunder 1999, 37). With Genesis in mind (Genesis 2:17), we can see that even though mankind had lost both the knowledge of God and the image of God; only by God's involvement can that broken relationship, intimacy and fellowship be fixed and completely restored.

(b) Still on page 37. In part XV, "For this reason was he born, appeared as man and died and rose again (from death) that whithersoever men have been lured away, he may recall from thence, and reveal to them his own true Father as he himself says, I came to seek and to save that which was lost" (Bettensen and Maunder 1999, 37). Regarding the theory of atonement, "by which the deceiver is deceived was first hinted at Ignatius of Antioch write up. The ruler of this age was deceived by the virginity of Mary, but the full story of the ransom and the bait is due to Gregory of Nyssa" (Bettensen and Mauder 1999, 37- 38). This Gregory of Nyssa or Gregory Nazianzus contributions on the defense of the gospel could be reached on Robert Louis Wilken's book, the Spirit of the Early Christian thought. Wilkens covered a lot concerning the defense on Christianity, making mention of some of the men involved and committed in this pursuit. Like Tertullian assurance in David Roper's book, giving assurance "that we shouldn't regret a thing which has been taken away and taken away by the Lord God, without whose will neither does a leaf glide down from a tree nor a sparrow of one farthing's worth fall to the earth" (Roper 2008, 135).

Remember that "everything that is believed is believed after being preceded by thought" (Wilkens 2003 XIII) and like Wilken said about Augustine Archbishop of Canterbury, "that like all great Christian thinkers, he consciously moved within a tradition he had himself not created" (Wilken 2003, XIII, XIX). The explanation regarding incarnation and atonement of Christ, will help erase any doubts in the minds of people, regarding any questions or complicated problems which may be holding both Christians and non-Christians back from receiving and believing in the authenticity or reality of the Bible.

Henry Bettensen & Chris Maunder stated that "the purpose of incarnation, was that the divine virtue of the son of God might be as it were a book hidden beneath the form of human flesh... to lure on the prince of this age to a contest; that the son might offer him his flesh as a bait and that then the divinity which lay beneath might catch him and hold him fast with its hook. Then as a fish when it seizes a baited hook not only fails to drag off the bait but it itself is dragged out of the water to serve as food for other. So, he that had the power of death seized the body of Jesus in death, unaware of the hook of divinity concealed therein. Having swallowed it, he was caught straight way, the bars of hell were burst and he was, as it were drawn up from the pit to become food for others" (Bettensen and Maunder 1999, 38). "Traditional theology had the support of Athanasius and Augustine for the view that the incarnation depended on the Fall and the church in her missal proclaimed the paradox of Adams transgression and its blessed consequence" (Bettensen and Mauder 1999, 156).

As commented on page 156 of Chris Maunder's third Ed., the why of the incarnation is revealed on pages 54 and 55 and I'll briefly quote in part, page 54, "for we could not overcome the author of sin and death, unless he had taken our nature and made it his own, whom sin could not defile nor death retain, since he was conceived of the Holy Spirit, in the womb of his Virgin Mother, whose virginity remained entire in his birth as in His conception" (Bettensen and Mauder 1999, 54). Hence in page 55, "the son of God therefore came down from His throne in heaven without withdrawing from His Father's glory and entered this lower world, born after a new order, by a new mode of birth. After a new order, since he is invisible in his own nature and He became visible in ours; He is incomprehensible, and he willed to be comprehended; continuing to be before time, he began to exist in time.... By a new mode of birth, in as much as virginity inviolate which knew not the desire of the flesh supplied the material of the flesh" (Bettensen and Mauder 1999,55). Furthermore, in page 52, "the natures which were brought together to form a true unity were different; but out of both is one Christ and one son" (Bettensen and Mauder 1999,52).

What a book; the names and the roles played by most of the Saints were reflected in Robert Louis Wilkens book, the Spirit of Early Christian Thought. Other contributors like Syriac writer, Jacob of Sarug, Justin the Martyr, John of Damascus, Chrysostom, John, all agreed that the bread represented the body of Christ and that the cup represented His blood. All these people agreed with Ignatius of Antioch in Syria. Hilary of Poitier answer to the question of resurrection was that "the Resurrection of Christ transfigured everything" (Wilkens 2003, 91). "No one except God can rise from death to life by its own power, writes Hilary" (Wilkens 2003, 91). Thomas, the apostle agreed to the resurrection. Wilken's book answered a lot of questions concerning the resurrection of Christ which is the dividing part in human history. "More often in the scriptures God is known through events that took place in history and the testimony of those who saw and heard the wondrous things that had happened" (Wilkens 2003, 176). One question asked which even I was not aware or sure of the right answer was, "why did Jesus not appear to those who had treated him despitefully and to those who condemned him and to everyone everywhere?" (Wilkens 2003, 181) This question came from Celsius who challenged the veracity of the resurrection of Jesus because all the witnesses where disciples. Origen of Alexandria answered succinctly that "Jesus appeared only to those who were capable of knowing what they were seeing" (Wilkens 2003, 181). That was a question and Origen provided a reasonable and immediate answer, that is the scriptural promised answer of God. Grace was always around the corner, to be sure. My thanks again go to Newburgh Theological Seminary for your recommended books.

Chapter seven of Wilkens book touched a very sensitive section of the scripture about reason and faith, that even Thomas Jefferson commented that the chain of that "monkish ignorance" should be broken, as earlier mentioned. It was a fact as Celsus echoed Galen's accusation that some Christians don't even want to give or receive a reason for what they believe and use expressions such as, "do not ask questions, just believe and your faith will save you". Reference was made about Paul playing down on the issue. "In the late eighteenth century an ancient French philosopher approach, gave reason, a new life". "At every moment of one's thinking, reason is accompanied by a word (Sermo) whatever you think takes the form of a word and whatever you imagine is reason" (Wilken 2003 98-99).

John's ministry was to prepare the nation for the coming of the Messiah by the rite of baptism, symbolic of cleansing of sin by the death of Jesus that was to come. Jesus identified Himself with the Jewish nation and takes upon Himself the obligation of keeping the whole law (613 laws). His baptism was so that John would have a revelation of His deity. By identifying Himself with those He came to redeem Jesus inaugurated His public ministry as the Messiah. There can be no doubt that all three persons of the Trinity are actively involved here as distinct persons of the Godhead. The Father speaks, the spirit descends and the son is baptized. This was the sign of Trinitarian agreement and confirmation. We must remember the significance of the gifts brought by the wise men which provided Joseph with the necessary funds to take his family to Egypt.

(1) The Gold signifies His Kingship.

(2) Frankincense signifies His priesthood.

(3) Myrrh an embalmer for death, symbolized His death for us. It was fitting, that Jesus begin His ministry as humanity's representative, with a mission to destroy the works of the devil, with victory over this adversary of the human race. The God who appeared in Christ was the same God who appeared to Abraham, Isaac, Jacob, Moses and Sarah.

Jesus has come to undo what happened in the garden. Eve and Adam, in the Garden of Eden committed three sins, 1st John 2:16. Jesus went through the three temptations to cancel or erase that evidence. Mathew 4:1-11 covered the temptation process.

(1) Turn the stones to bread (Lust of the flesh).

(2) Jump off the temple (pride of life).

(3) Fall down and worship me (lust of eyes). Jesus' answer teaches us that we need to know the word of God. Study it, believe it, and practice it, and be able to enforce it as needed. Be committed

in your willingness to trust and obey. Trust and obey, for there is no other way to be happy in Jesus but to trust and obey, a song by John Henry Sammis. Trust and obey are the two wings of the Christian, one without the other ends in nothing. Obedience and faith, trust being one side of the coin and obedience, the other said A.W. Tozer in his book, Experiencing the presence of God, page 61. He brought us to focus on how we lost our relationship with God because of the shift in moral order, resulting in moral bankruptcy of the human soul, page 18. He writes, "man inevitable striking against the kingdom of God and the moral order and becomes a debt to the great God who created heavens and earth. The good news, however, is that Christ has paid the debt and bridged that gap to God for all" (Tozer 2010, 18). This is where my dissertation kicks in showing how we can go from where we are to where we ought to be. Knowing this from the true Holy Bible, all What God has said and done, How He has said and did it, and Why He said and did it, gives us the revealed knowledge to know how to do it God's way. Before this discovery we,

(a) were slaves to sin.

(b) were heirs of misery, pain sickness, death and poverty, and giving birth to children, not for God but for the glory and joy of the devil.

(c) had no legal approach to God. He was not our Father Romans 7:24- 25, Hebrew 2:14-15. It was after all these that Colossians 2:14-15 took effect, Ephesians 2:12-13.

So, your redeemer must be one over who Satan has no legal claim or authority over Him. In conclusion of these Christ temptations, what was outstanding in this temptation was the answers Christ gave in the three questions Satan came up with, "it is written", Matthew 4:6, 7, 10. The answers to your questions are already there. This is how we who are practicing Christians ought to respond. This is the dissertations intentions to let the practicing and non-practicing Christians to understand that what they are looking up to receive is at the eye-level. We are moving from Numbers 21:9 to Acts 16:31, 1st Peter 2:24. From this event Jesus declared that all that have been written were written about Him both Old Testament Psalm 40:7 and New Testament, Hebrews 10:7. Whatever God has spoken, every pronouncement, every declaration and every promise, are based on His capability, availability and willingness.

There are lots and lots of promised answers and promised solutions, examples shown on How to tackle issues biblically, or scripturally. The ball is in your court. Change your thinking and change your life. The believers should start believing and trusting God, the source of all need, the master of all need, Jesus has come to answer them all. The partakers should start partaking in the Holy Communion in remembrance of the death, burial and resurrection of our Lord Jesus Christ. Believers should start believing. Remember that faith will not kick in until the Will of God is known. And what is the Will of God, find it as it is written. Find out what is written and you will be there with the scriptural promised answers and scripturally promised solutions. There are examples of the 'How' you can apply this to ugly situations and be free. Every practicing believer has the privilege and benefit of direct access to God, 1st Peter 2:9 with this we are called to a lifestyle that honor and bring glory to Him.

The Beatitudes or Sermon on the Mount. This is covered in Matthew Chapters 5 to 7. In summary,

(1) This is the theology of Christianity and is regarded as the Lord's constitution.

(2) The Beatitudes are the government that is founded on the principles of the kingdom.

(3) It spells out what is required of a believer.

(4) The commandments of Jesus are His laws and His statutes.

(5) It is a statement of Policy, and practice for those who belong to the kingdom of Heaven.

(6) Jesus stressed that a relationship with God is an inward attitude, and not an outward ritual. It's all about you been blessed = happy; about Love, Joy, Peace, Forgiveness, Forget and Ignore. The art of being wise is the art of knowing what to ignore, as written by many Christian writers.

Your desire to please God glorifies and brings honor to him. You can't serve God without knowing Him for real, working/walking with Him, its only then and then only can you serve Him. That's why Jesus told the disciples in John 15:15-16 that they are now friends and that He has ordained them to work with Him for the benefit of the kingdom. This process of teaching the disciples was the power behind their success after He has departed and His Will applied. He explained to them, concerning the spirit, soul and body, 1st Thessalonians 5:23. He explained to them that humans are spirit being, they possess a soul and live in a physical body. "The soul has three compartments, the Will, the Mind, and the Emotions. The mind harbors the compartment that chooses, that feels and thinks. It is observed that whatever or whoever controls the mind, controls the emotion and controls the individual. Joyce Meyer's book, The Battlefield of the Mind, illustrated this aspect very well. Andrew Wommack in his book, Spirit Soul & Body also wrote extensively on the role of the mind. The Bible alerts us to the fact that there are two aspects of the world. We enter the invisible; The Kingdom of God, when we become born again. We are citizens of the invisible world. Jesus told them the difference between the kingdom of God, which is the kingdom of the Father, the Son and Holy Spirit and the kingdom of Heaven.

The kingdom of God is governed by spiritual laws as well as physical laws. Ignorance of God's laws will not protect you from Satan's traps or temptations. God is not a respecter of persons nor do the laws. He reminded them that to have meaning, life must have a purpose, Jeremiah 29:11. There has been built into creation a cycle of rest and work, the sanctity of the home, the necessity of truthfulness, sacredness of property rights, the destructiveness of envy, the value of life. Jesus tells what will ease hostilities and enable us to live in peace. He touched on unity and on our willingness to become what he has created us to be. He also reminded them that situation do not create your character, they reveal it. He advised them to avoid hypocrisy. He went out to highlight the Golden Rule Matthew 7:12 for every action there is a corresponding reaction. This is the law of nature and bears the command for you to love your neighbor as yourself. Your neighbor is the one with a need, whose need you can visualize and whose need you can also meet. Your willingness to be an answer to someone's need, that's the neighbor the bible is talking about.

God had already met our basic needs.

(1) Acceptance: knowing that you are loved and appreciated and needed by people, Ephesians 1:6.

(2) Security: Knowing that you are provided for and protected from. Give others a push of encouragement, Psalms 91:1-16.

(3) Identity: Knowing that you are an individual, significant and special, wonderfully and fearfully made with gifts and talents to fit, Psalm 139:14.

(4) Purpose: Knowing that you have a reason for living and that God has a special plan and purpose for you, Jeremiah 29:11.

(5) Our relationship with God in now assured. The intimacy and fellowship guaranteed.

With this relationship, there is freedom as seen in Psalms 91:1-3 and as WM Paul Young said, "Freedom is a process that happens inside a relationship with the Lord" (Young 2007, 95). "It is not intolerant or unloving to say that the bible is the solution to, not the source of the problem", Whitney T Kuniholm once President of the Scripture Union said that.

Chapters 8 to 9 is about Miracles. This is Jesus presenting His credentials to the nation, manifesting His power as proof of His Messiahship. He showed the Messiah's power over diseases, nature, demons and death. This is handing over period, teaching and testing has now started. In Chapter 10, here He called the twelve disciples and gave them power and authority to deal with unclean spirits, to cast them out, to heal all manner of sickness and all manner of diseases. The parables were illustrated but the most striking was the parable of the Sower. The question by the disciples as to why He spoke in parables were explained along with the meaning, purpose and significance of the parable of the sower. This was the key to understanding all other parables. All the questions asked by the disciples were carefully answered, and the how and the why carefully explained. He reminded them that the right and proper understanding of the what, how and why of the Bible was very necessary and that our evangelism should start with explanation of the whys of the Bible. He answered and thoroughly taught them how to pray, telling them that he used parables because of the Pharisees who rejected Him and that parables teaches heavenly truth by using an earthly illustration.

Jesus taught in parables to show what would happen in His absence between the time of His going back to Heaven and His return which was at hand. He stated that all the Gospel seeds sown will not bear fruit, good and evil will exist side by side until His second coming. This is the Dualism mentioned by C.S. Lewis stating, that "equal and independent powers are at the back of everything, one of them good and the other bad" (Lewis 1980, 42); and warning that "if you do not take the distinction between good and bad very seriously, then it is easy to say that anything you find in this world is a part of God" (Lewis 1980, 37). Good must be defined scripturally, per how Prof. Millard J. Erickson defined it saying, "Good is to be defined in relationship to the will and being of God" (Erickson 1998, 450). Jesus' entire ministry was about changing people's perception about God the Father, and that's how you bring your life to line up with the word of God. Remember that the Bible is written with the spiritual aspect of it in mind. This is how you become a practicing Christian.

The parables are intended to show the growth and development of the church during this dispensation, its relation to sinners, to those who profess to be Christians, and to the world in general. There was a total of thirteen parables. Chapter 17 dealt with transfiguration of Jesus. Why was this event important? The explanation:

(1) Moses represented the Old Testament law.

(2) Elijah represented the Old Testament prophets.

(3) Moses and Elijah disappeared and only Jesus was left, only Grace was left.

(4) This illustration was that notice should no longer be taken of the Old Testament law or prophets, but of the New Testament prophet and King, Jesus.

Chapters 24 and 25 are two of the most misunderstood passages as they concern only the Jews, and not Christians. Chapters 26-28 concerns the arrest, trial, death and resurrection of the King. This closes with the Great Commission. All these go to point out the authenticity of the bible and the assurance that your questions and solutions where anticipated and scriptural promised answers and scriptural promised solution had been made available. The book Taming your Mind by Ken Keyes alerts us always to remember "that the value of this book lies not in how well you can talk about it, but rather in the changes for better it makes in your own thinking habits as shown in your day to day actions and problems solving" (Keyes 1975, 34). "Edison said, Genius is 1% inspiration and 99% perspiration" (Keyes 1975, 34) "To read without reflecting is like eating without digesting" (Keyes 1975, 34) as Ken Keyes Jr. said. Also, H.L Wayland said "that the only people who make no mistakes are dead people", page 52. "If Christianity is reduced to a doctrine that can be explained with no intuitive knowledge, no direct knowledge of the heart of God, then where is the wonder of it?" (Tozer 2010, 81) so asked A.W. Tozer. Tozer also said that "The Bible and nature bear the same signature upon them, so that we can conclude that whoever made one, made the other" (Tozer 2010, 85).

It is noted that from the human point of view there is no solutions for the conflict of interest in the world. Leaders are naturally afraid, sick and tired and even frustrated in trying to deal with increasing problems in the society, but with God all things are possible, all questions have scriptural promised answers and all problems have scriptural promised solutions for those who believe. For this, it is now extremely important for Christians to be actively involved in government so that the government's values are consistent with the word of God. This is what Stephen McDowell and Mark Beliles' book, 'Liberating the Nations' are emphasizing, that we must keep our eyes and mind open to recognize important changes and be ready for adjustments and course corrections, as and when due. They concluded that "How we educate our youths have immeasurable consequences for the future of our nation" (McDowell and Beliles 1995, 105). This is biblical, Mathew 15:21-28.

Chapter 13

Mark's Account

Mark is the gospel of miracles and to me most appealing to American minds. Brief, short sentences, blunt to the point, short and sweet are taken into consideration. A gospel of action and accomplishment, written most primarily for large Gentile audience resident in Rome. Written in the present tense is focused on what Jesus does rather than what He says. Jesus' example of service is pointed out as the pattern for all His followers, Mark 16:20. There is no genealogy of Christ in this book. It's worth to look at the central theme of this Gospel of Mark, Mark 10:41-45.

(1) There is no sense that the son of God is the servant of God, nor that we being the sons of God, are the servants of God.

(2) Spiritually, we are sons of God, but in our physical body, we are servants to bring the Gospel to the people.

(3) Jesus is our example of how we ought to act towards our fellow man.

So, we can conclude here like the Mark outlook wrote, that the Gospel is concerned to his target. Jesus life ministry and passion is Christocentric and action oriented. The first section, chapters 1-9 deals with the son of man ministering and chapters 10-16, the son of man giving His life as a ransom. Close look at Isaiah presenting Jesus as the suffering servant of God Isaiah 42:1 connects Mark 10:45. The most outstanding chapter that deals closely with my dissertation is in Chapter 5 of Marks Gospel. This deals with what He did to what happened. How He handled it and why. After Jesus has settled the storm and leaving His disciples wondering what manner of man He was, He increased their surprise and confusion by settling yet a demon possessed Gadarene man. Jesus was going to answer a call concerning Jairus' daughter who was sick and at the point of death, when He was interrupted. This ruler of the synagogue, Jairus believed that if Jesus could come to his house to see the daughter everything will be alright.

So, Jesus was going to Jairus house when someone intercepted. The woman with the issue of blood. This woman just burst out onto Jesus. A lot of lesson lies here. What happens in between? Here I believe and here I receive. What did Jesus do and how did He handle it and why? What is common to the two individuals involved, if not belief. It was pure belief and un-diluted and uncontaminated belief. Jairus believed and the woman also believed. Jairus daughter represented the new generation and the woman who represented the bleeding church, must be healed first, before the incoming generation. This woman had heard that Jesus was coming and passing by and she said, if I may touch but his clothes I shall be made whole. Faith cometh by hearing and hearing by the word of God, Romans 10:17. She may have been aware of Malachi 4:2 and armed with these words she concluded that this is the day which the Lord hath made, and that she will rejoice and be glad in it, Psalms 118:24. With this knowledge she defiled all protocols and gave voice to the power of God knowing that the power of God is voice activated. Her belief produced the corresponding action she took. That was How the woman was healed. She enforced the law of healing, 1st Peter 2:24. She knew what has been said, applied the law of How and agreed and believed the Why she shouldn't fail and started off to break all protocols to achieve her desired goal. She knew what she ought to say, how she ought to say it, and believe it, and why she ought to believe and then place a demand.

She must enforce it to happen accordingly and immediately, instantly she was made whole and the flow of blood stopped. What next, Jesus asked, who touched me? Why? because He observed and felt that virtue had gone out of Him. The woman fearing and trembling shows up to say what has happened and Jesus concluded, and said to her, daughter thy faith hath made thee whole, go in peace and be whole of thy plaque. This shows that God works silently secretly and supernaturally to those who will believe and refuse to doubt the scriptural promises of God which must come to pass. This woman showed up in between and Jesus was there and showed out in between to sort out the woman's problem who has been suffering many years from the hands of physicians and other health workers. In summary, can you say it to yourself like the woman did in Mark 5:27-28? Can you voice it out to enforce it and receive it as if her healing had already been decreed? Can you act like the woman did to defend your healing as in Mark 5:33? Faith will not work if the will of God is not known. The woman's faith caused her to receive what she wanted. She made use of the power of 'Now', The Power of Now by Eckhart Tolle. The woman acted immediately right there not wasting any moment to get herself healed. While Jesus was about stepping out of this event the news that Jairus daughter had died was released and immediately Jesus speaks out to Jairus. Be not afraid, only believe. Jesus did this to avoid doubts, unbelief, and fear which could have contaminated the man's faith. He only took the father and the mother along with Peter, James and John and went into the place where the damsel was lying. Jesus, raised her back to life (revivification) and handed the damsel over to her parents and their joy was completed. We can see the power of belief and unbelief. Jesus could not heal anyone in His own home town of Nazareth because of their unbelief. This is covered excellently by Mark 5:21-43.

Putting out unbelievers wasn't a new thing. Elijah did it. Elisha, Peter all did it to enforce the power of God. The unbelief issue and its opposite twin brother, belief, reside within same compartment. Doubt is what supports unbelief. Unbelief is refusal to trust God's word. Fear of obstacles and seeing the problems and not God. With

God, nothing is impossible and now that Jesus is on earth and with Jesus Christ nothing will also be impossible for Him to tackle.

(1) Noah believed that he heard from God and started building the ark, Genesis 6:4.

(2) Abraham believed, acted and gave birth to a nation, Genesis 12:2.

(3) Moses acted and brought 2-3 million souls out of slavery, Exodus 3:10.

(4) The blind man acted and received his sight, Luke 18:42.

(5) The man with the withered arm acted and was healed, Mark 3:1-6.

(6) Rahab acted and saved her own family, Joshua 6:25.

(7) The woman with the issue of blood believed, acted and received healing, Luke 8:44.

(8) The woman bound by Satan for 18 years, healed on a Sabbath day, Luke 13:12. All these go to show like "Grotius revealed, that man can only be truly self-governed if his reason, will, and appetite are ruled by God. The basis of self-control is obedience to the creator and His standards of conduct found in the Bible" (McDowell and Beliles 1995, 7).

Jesus is now on His Father's business. Doing what is required, showing and demonstrating how and why the Father wanted it done. Fulfilling the Old testament prophesies and laws demonstrating righteous anger in cleansing of the temple and the power of faith in the event of the fig tree. Jesus answers to most of the implicating questions like, paying taxes, tribute to Caesar, the Sadducees and resurrection left the righteous people confused. Mark 13, speaks of

Tribulation. Chapters 14 and 15 speaks of Jesus' last hours. Healing on a Sabbath day angered the religious people and attracted envy and jealousy.

Mark 14: 32-36, shows that in those dark hours when Jesus needed human sympathy and companionship, rather it was human nature at work. He had to brace his body, nerve his soul and calm His spirit by prayer and solitude so that He could confront what lay ahead. You can see the abuse on Jesus by the Jewish and Roman law. The purpose of the trials (three before the Jewish authorities and three before Roman authorities) was to find a legal basis on which Jesus could be condemned to death, Mark 14:53-65. Since the Jews did not have the authority to put Jesus to death they must seek the order of Roman authority, Mark 15:1. Jesus submission to this entire procedure is the measure of His total submission to the will of God 15:16-20. His crucifixion is covered by Mark 15:33-41. The death, the burial and resurrection of Jesus is the power of God. Know the purpose and the significance of this resurrection power of God. When Jesus arrived, the facts and the reality became one in him. The seen and the unseen became one. The invisible became visible, and that is why He said in John 14:6 that He is the way, the truth and the life, and that if you have seen Him, you have also seen the Father, John 14:8-9.

In conclusion of Mark's account in Chapter 16,

(a) the disciples were bewildered and felt total despair when Jesus died on the cross.

(b) they were confused and fearful, which prevented them from believing in the possibility of the resurrection.

(c) when they finally believed they became dynamic witnesses.

(d) the reality of the resurrection of Jesus from the dead set them free, the central message of the resurrection is "Be not affrighted…he is risen" Mark 16:6.

(e) after the resurrection, the world was still the same, but the disciples were different because the risen Christ had changed them as He does us from the inside out.

(f) the resurrection, the cornerstone of all Christian faith, is Christ's Victory.

Jesus appeared twelve times after Resurrection per the scriptures. Jesus charge to His disciples and His ascension Mark 16:14-20, Have faith in God, Mark 11:22-24. And remember that all things are possible with God, Mark 10:27. If all things are possible with God, it then means all problems have proven scriptural promised solutions and every issue in one's life has scriptural promised answers and solutions. Remember that all these issues are covered by the atonement, and be aware that stealing, fear, unbelief are not covered by the atonement. It's our responsibility to knock them down.

Chapter 14
Luke's Account

Luke's message is uniquely fresh, attractive and compelling. Luke stresses the overarching plan of God in human history as revealed through Israel, Christ and the church. He puts special emphasis on salvation and calls special attention to children, the poor and disreputable as recorded in the introductory section of the gospel. The Bible records show that four groups of people were touched by Jesus, during his period on earth while doing his Father's business,

(1) the Gentiles

(2) the Samaritans,

(3) the Women

(4) the Poor. Words and scenes are here recorded that are not in the other books.

    (a) The parents of John the Baptist.

    (b) The two encounters with the angel Gabriel.

    (c) The visit of Mary to Elizabeth.

    (d) The birth of John the Baptist.

    (e) The prophecy of Zacharias and other special events.

This gospel was written primarily for the Greeks who were especially interested in the ideal man. Luke was called the beloved physician and was the companion of Paul at various times. He was a true historian and gives dates which can be checked. Luke 1:5, 2:1, 3:1-2, 23. Several of his parables could only be found in Luke's gospel. Luke begins with joy and ended with Joy. Luke 1:13-14. And Luke 24:52. Women also have a special place in Luke's gospel – the beginning of Christian care for women. Examples

(a) Anna the prophetess

(b) the woman of Nain

(c) the woman who was a sinner but whose love was great.

(d) Mary and Martha.

(e) the weeping daughter of Jerusalem.

Dr. Gary R. Collins wrote that "we prepare for the future by anchoring ourselves in basic Christian values and beliefs, taking the time to know God better, listening for his voice, and becoming like the open-minded people of Berea. They listened carefully to messages that might be from God and searched the scriptures so they could discern what was true" (Collins 2007, 848).

Prayer has a special place in Luke's narrative. How did Jesus handle the issue of prayer? Luke emphasized in prayer, knowing it is one communication device to dialogue with God. A lot of people have written on prayer, how to pray, better way to pray and so on. People like A.W. Tozer, Andrew Wommack (Writing on a Better Way to Pray), Dr. Tony Evans, and Dr. Kevin J Conner to name a few have written on prayers, how we ought and ought not to pray. What is prayer and what is not prayer. What is the Bible saying about it?

Whatever you say or do will be weighed against what God has said and done. How you say or do things must be weighed against how God said and did it. Why you say or do things have also to be weighed against why God said it or did it. Everything about the kingdom is governed by laws. God's laws of What, How and Why. One may ask what is law? Law is an established principle that will work for anyone who applies it irrespective of human differences. In the court system, Judges apply this principle to find out why someone has done or committed any crime. Did he or she go against the laws that has been established? What are the intentions, the motives for doing things?

All what God has said and done, all how God has said and done them, and all why God has said and done them are all governed by laws. This was why Paul in Ephesians 1:17-18 was telling them that his request from God was that He would give them the spirit of wisdom to acknowledge what God has said and done, the revelation knowledge of how to scripturally / biblically do things and understanding the why of God, the reasons for God's doings. In science, also, there are principles of how to analyze stuff and there are what we call the SOPs that is Standard Operational Procedures. You must follow an already established principles tried and confirmed. So, science through God has made these things available to us to follow per What, How and Why of God.

That's why Ephesians 3:20 and 2nd Corinthians 1:20 are written to assure you of God's promises. Many people have defined success as this or that but when you look at Robert E. Logan's definition of success, it agrees with my dissertation pursuit regarding the "what" of God in his book 'Beyond Church Growth'. His definition of success is very simple. "Find out what it is that God wants you to do, and then do it" (Logan 1989, 30). Find out God's purpose, what He has created you to do. Ask the questions Why and How and get the answers you need for you to succeed.

Robert. E. Logan, went on to say, "It is exciting to realize that God has granted us the authority to open human eyes so that they may perceive the absolute reality of heavenly truth" (Logan 1989, 26). Another striking event was the cleansing of a leper in Luke 5:12-16, which was also dealt with in Mathew 8:3. This man who was a leper said to Jesus, 'Lord if thou wilt, thou canst make me clean'. This man did not doubt Jesus capability or His availability since he was face to face with Jesus. The leper knew Jesus as the Messiah, understood the power of his words, Romans 4:17. He knew that God's words created the heavens and the earth and like Pastor Lawson Perdue wrote in his book, the Power and Life of the Word, he stated that "what he speaks creates and changes reality to confirm to His words. When he calls something that is not as though it was, the word he spoke releases power to change the situation" (Lawson 2014, 17). The power of God is always voice activated.

The doubt the leper had in his mind was if Jesus was willing to heal him. Jesus put forth His hand and touched the leper saying, 'I will, be thou healed'. We are assured of His willingness to meet our needs, as "God's guidance stems from our relationship with Him" (Banks 2014, 22).

This is what my dissertation is all about, that God has assured us and demonstrated His capability, His availability and His willingness to meet our needs if we believe and trust Him. Healing the man was another show of Jesus willingness to demonstrate God's intention for all who are willing to trust Him, 2nd Peter 3:9. From this incident Jesus assured us that faith can be understood as written in Luke 5:20 He said to the man, your sin is forgiven. This statement did not go well with the religious people and the Pharisees who started to inquire who Jesus is as to speak blasphemy and say he has the right to forgive one's sins which only God could do. Jesus asked them which one they will accept, whether to say your sins are forgiven or to say, arise, pick up thy couch and go. Jesus asserted His deity and said to the man arise and take up thine couch and go into thine house. Immediately he arose before all of them, took all that belonged to him and left, glorifying God. He showed them that He, Jesus has the power on earth to forgive sin. He healed on a Sabbath day and defended His disciples who entered the house of God and ate the shew bread? Jesus demonstrated His power and His desire in bringing both the Jews and the Gentiles together, treating them as one. He healed the centurion's servant, and raised the son of a widow. He did stress the power of love, the importance of counting the cost regarding following Him.

Jesus demonstrated His deity, His divine relationship with God showing that what He says creates what He does and how He says it becomes how He did it, and why He said it becomes the reason why He did it. It's all about how you ought to trust and obey. There is no higher honor than to be invited to follow the son of God, but you must count the cost. There are three types of people, those

(a) who are quick to follow.

(b) who are slow to follow

(c) who are undecided, Luke 9:57-62.

Jesus was very good at spoiling Satan's plans and replacing them with God's will. Jesus reiterated the power over enemies readily available for the disciples' use. At all points, God's willingness is demonstrated. Chapter 15 deals with the parable of the lost sheep. Luke15:1-7, lost coin Luke 15:8-10 and the parable of the prodigal son Luke15:11-32. In all these Jesus explained the purpose and significance of each parable. Bear in mind that a lost coin is out of circulation and therefore useless. The sheep can be killed by the lions.

The prodigal son illustrated the heart of the father towards rebellious children and the anxiety, urgency and expectation for the return of His son. God is ready to forgive us. Remember Luke 9: 51- Luke 19:44 are details of Jesus final journey to Jerusalem. These are not found in any other gospel. The parable of the unrighteous steward narrated in Luke 16:1-15 shocked even me. How can Jesus commend an unrighteous steward? He was proving a case. He changed from being selfish to taking care of others. Self-centeredness was condemned and since he was now using the money wisely, he was pardoned instead of attracting condemnation. He was pardoned and forgiven.

So, Jesus made four points for us to take home.

(1) People of this world are clever in accomplishing their self-centered ambitions; they are cleverer in gaining worldly wealth than Christians are in gaining spiritual understanding (wealth).

(2) Jesus advised His followers to use their money to win new converts so they will be warmly welcomed into God's eternal home; even as the shrewd steward used his resources to gain friends and be welcomed into their home.

(3) Jesus stated that the true test of character is revealed on how you handle money. If a person is faithful in small things; he will be equally faithful in larger things. The issue of the rich, young ruler of 18:18-27 was brought up and Jesus said, it was a question of trust; God loves to be trusted, Proverbs 13:11. Ray Stedman in his Discovery Series, states that "Christianity would never have survived, if it were based on lies" (Stedman 2016, 16).

(4) Jesus made it plain that no one can be truly faithful to God and mammon at the same time. No one is expected to be a part time Christian. Trusting God with your money is the least area of trust. Jesus talked more on money because He knows that money can easily become our master and not our servant. Dr. Creflo Dollar in one of his TV sermon said that trust is the issue and emphasized that learning to trust God starts with one's finances and concluded by saying that nothing is impossible for those who trust God. Yes, I agree with him because God does

not need your apology but expect that His goodness towards you will produce a repentant heart in you, 2nd Peter 3:9.

Chapter 18:15-17 dealt with Jesus and children and chapter 19:10 is regarded as the key verse of the book of Luke. For the son of man is come to seek and save that which is lost. Chapter 24 deals with disciples after the resurrection and Jesus ascension to the father. Chapter 18:1-8 dealt with the widow and the judge which illustrates a contrast and not a comparison. God does not delay answering prayer regarding your needs when you cry for genuine help, Chapter 18:9-14 deals with self-righteousness. The widow and the judge is a sure example of where Christians also instead of seeing it as a contrast is taking it as if you must continue bombarding God until something happens, that is to continue praying until something happens (P.U.S.H), in Luke 18:8, see how it is answered. We must mark where it's used as a comparison, where it is used as an example, where it is used to contrast or where it is used in a wishful manner, if not, you will wrongly interpret the intentions of the writer. Pray until your sense of peace returns and not pray until something happens. The Bible interprets itself, read the whole context before concluding, if not, when you remove the text, you will be left with con. The Bible reminds us that we should use our mind to do the work for which God has created us to do and not allow our mind to use us for meeting the requirement of our flesh.

Chapter 15
John's Account

John's gospel came on an entirely different plan and was written many years after the three gospels of Mathew, Mark and Luke. John having in mind the needs of Christians, of all nations presents a deeper truth of the gospel, the deity of Jesus Christ and the Holy Spirit. Jesus is presented as the son of God. John's lifestyle was probably the same as that of Jesus. He would have spent time in the Jewish synagogue receiving instructions in Jewish custom and laws. John and Andrew were disciples of John the Baptist and when they heard John the Baptist comment on Jesus, 'Behold the Lamb of God' they turned and began to follow Jesus. So, John is the author of the gospel of John written at the end of the first century. This is followed by the 1st, 2nd, and 3rd John and then the book of Revelation. His writings were done in Ephesus. The churches we read about, Smyrna Pergamos, Thyatira, Sardis, Philadelphia and Laodicea, were founded by John. When John and James became aware that Jesus was the expected Messiah, they abandoned their fishing business and followed Jesus. Jesus made John one of His disciples and He became one of the inner circles along with James and Peter. John was with Jesus during the great crisis in His life, the agony in Gethsemane and the transfiguration also. He was recognized as one who was closest to Jesus, the disciple whom He loves. John took Mary away after the crucifixion and cared for her the rest of her life.

Here again it is what Jesus said and did, how He said and did it and the why of it all. Since John was very intimate with Jesus; his main reason for writing the gospel is to show us that Jesus is the son of God, who came in the flesh. Jesus revealed a lot to John and as such was called John the revelator. It was in revelation Chapter 4:11 that Johns words revealed the song that came out of the heart of the Israelites after crossing the Red sea. John gave witness and recorded the words and works of Jesus, that revealed His divine power and glory. John is more elevated in tone and more exalted in view than the other gospels. Jesus deity is revealed in every chapter of John. Jesus was challenged to prove Himself, show evidence to validate what He claims to be. If your claim is genuine, then show yourself to the world. You don't hide yourself and expect people to know you, John 7:3-4. Prove yourself to be worthy, 2nd Timothy 2:15. Jesus claimed that His ability to teach should prove the divine origin of His message, John 7:15. Obedience helps to determine true doctrine, John 7:17.

John revealed a lot about Jesus deity and why it was necessary for Him to come down. Many other people have written but here I will refer to Eckhart Tolle contribution to this issue. Tolle wrote that, "Humans have been in the grip of pain for eons, or for a very long time, ever since they fell from the state of grace, entered the realm of time and mind, and lost awareness of Being. At that point, they started to perceive themselves as meaningless fragments in an alien universe, unconnected to the source and to each other" (Tolle 1999, 25). Tolle also mentioned that "emotion being part of Dualistic mind is subject to the law of opposites. This simply means that you cannot have good without bad" (Tolle 1999, 24). Having eaten from the tree of the knowledge of good and evil and love having been replaced by conscience did set in motion, a chain of reactions not easy to stop or counter balance easily. Only God knew how we got here and only God can supply the how to get us out from there. God of All in All, knows the how and He did apply it as and when due to redeem us.

There are reasons for and against acceptance and rejection of Jesus which John 7:25-52 took care of. One of God's purpose since the beginning has been to dwell with humanity and enjoy fellowship with us. Under this dispensation, He did it through the Holy Spirit, by the following five steps.

(1) The indwelling of the Holy Spirit.

(2) It's coming automatically as you are saved by your belief and acceptance, Romans 10:9-10. It is not an experience but produces spiritual experiences.

(3) It's remaining permanently.

(4) It becomes the basis of all other ministries.

(5) It being a source of new life in the believer.

Paraphrasing A.W. Tozer "that man is a moral criminal before the bar of God" (Tozer 2010, 58), some sort of reconciliation must be made before the return of fellowship. "This is what the Bible teaches and anything else is less than Bible doctrine" (Tozer 2010, 58).

Now we must recall that in the Garden of Eden there were two trees, the tree of life and the tree of knowledge of good and evil. I have already written about this, quoting Lois E. Lebar's book, Education that is Christian, page 151. Remarks by Andrew Murray. Looking at these two trees they represent two foundations scripturally. These foundations are based on your choice. God at creation established laws that will govern His creation. since God has created us in His own image after their likeness, He did create man along with the moral law or creation law as some writers call it, to test man's ability to resist or not to resist eating from the tree of good and evil. That is why we are sustained by the creative power of His spirit, whether we obey or disobey, the choice is yours. So, this gives the two foundations.

(1) Based on the foundation of resisting the temptation.

(2) Disobeying God and eating from the tree of good and evil which is the foundation based on being dominated by your sensory

mechanism; taste, smell, feel, sight, hearing as stated.

The issue of the Samaritan woman at the well, did fit into this scenario, John 4:18. Her marriages were based on sensory mechanism on how it tastes, how it smells and all failed. Since we are in seed form in Adam, we arrive at birth spiritually dead and so needed a Savior to deliver us from Adam's disobedience. We need to be regenerated because we were wrongly generated and as such regeneration of our nature is a necessity.

God first touch on us was at creation and a second touch was now necessary to redeem us form sin brought up by Adam and that touch was the touch of redemption which was necessary to avoid our going to hell. It becomes necessary since your going to hell will now depend on your rejecting Christ's payment of atonement, John 14:6. Jesus came down and paid the debt we couldn't pay through his sacrifice and said just believe and receive the free gift of salvation, free gift of faith giving us everything pertaining to life and godliness, 2nd Peter 1:3. The choice is yours, Deuteronomy 30:19 and Joshua 24:15. Two foundations as Oswald Chambers commented in the book by Lois Lebar is that "the inner reality of redemption is that it creates all the time" (Lebar 1995, 212). As the redemption creates the life of God in us, so it creates the things belonging to that life. Nothing can satisfy the need but that which created the need. This is the meaning of Redemption; it creates and it satisfies". Which foundation are you on? Foundation based on Jesus Christ, Ephesians 2:20 or the foundation based on the universal standard of five senses, 2nd Corinthians 4:18. Jesus, the seen and the unseen, facts and reality, came to answer the unanswered question of How we ought to do stuff. So, we must be aware of what command we are obeying. That's why we must scripturally renew the spirit of our mind, Ephesians 4:23, since our "mind is the battlefield", and who is in control becomes an issue, a necessary question to be answered. Many have written on the issue of the mind, like I had mentioned earlier.

Whatever it may be, Eckhart Tolle had this to say about the mind; "Identification with your mind creates an opaque screen of concepts, labels, images, words, judgements and definitions that blocks all true relationship. It comes between you and yourself, between you and your fellow man and woman, between you and nature, between you and God" (Tolle 1999, 12). Concluding this aspect of the mind he said that "the mind cannot forgive" (Tolle 1999, 100) and that was the reason why Jesus said that before you enter the temple, check to see if there's any unforgiveness within which you must forgive, Matthew 5:23-24. Tolle said that "the moment you truly forgive, you have reclaimed power from the mind" (Tolle 1999, 100). "The mind is a superb instrument if used rightly. Used wrongly, however, it becomes very destructive" (Tolle 1999, 13).

All these were possible because Christ arrived the earth with detached seed of Sin. Just unlike the first Adam he could fulfill Mathew 5:17 successfully. Jesus stressed this connection between how the world ought to relate to God and how it would in turn relate to Christ's true followers, John 15:18.

The three keys to open the book of John. John 20:31, "but these are written that you might believe that Jesus is the Christ, the son of God and that believing you might have life through His Name". John chapter 16:28, "I came forth from the father and have come into the world. Again, I leave the world and go to the father". John 1: 11-12, "He came unto his own and his own received Him not. But as many as received Him to them gave He power to become the sons of God even to them that believe His Name". It was John who revealed what individuals thought about Christ in chapters 1-5.

What Christ said about himself in Chapters 11-20. Jesus revealed the secret of Christian life to His disciples. People were divided about Jesus identity and their unbelief developed into open and actual hostility. Jesus revealed who He was when He healed the blind man in chapter 9:1-12, regarding a man who was born blind. He discussed at length on the good shepherd in chapter 10. John brings a lot of witnesses to prove the deity of Christ. Numbers 23:19, Exodus 3:14, John 1:34, John 14:6, John 20:28, John 6:69. John must have enjoyed the simple pleasure of looking at our Lord, whom he loved and this is what we enjoy each time we worship God. We bask in His presence. There is always a lack or a default in any doctrine that focuses only on what we can gain from God but, the thing we were created and redeemed to do is to worship Him (Revelations 4:11). This takes us back to how and why. It's all about the 'How' and 'Why' in the Bible. If you master the 'Hows' and the 'Whys' of the Bible, any of your questions and problems will attract the scriptural answers and solutions. So master God's signature tune. Remember He has said in Psalms 84:11 that He will not withhold any good thing from those who walk uprightly and that believes and trusts Him. He concludes with Psalm 23 that "surely, goodness and mercy shall follow those who believe in Him and continue dwelling in the house of the Lord forever", Psalms 91:1-3. These are promises of God and are for those who believe in the finished work of Christ. Some of the statements are given as examples of how you can get to the bottom of your questions and problems. The how is seen in Hebrews 5:14, "but strong meat belong to them that are of full age, even those who by reason of use have their senses exercised to discern both good and evil". In Hebrews 10:22, its showing us how we can draw nearer to God so that He can draw near to us. Jesus was great enough to deserve our obedience, yet humble enough to call us friends, John 15:15.

God's desire to redeem believers cannot be frustrated because He is infinitely greater than any potential enemy. His plan will be realized because it's His purpose. His power is in His purpose, Romans 8:28. He created us on purpose for His purpose. "God gives us certain internal and external characteristics that enable us to fulfill our God-given purpose and call" (McDowell and Beliles 1995, 26). So, you are custom made. A wish from Paul to the Philippians as also a wish as John was addressing Gaius in 3 John 2 who has shown an exemplary lifestyle, opening his house to missionaries, comforting them and assisting them. Many are using it as a promise and not as a wish. John was expressing gratitude for his kindness and wishing that he would continue to experience God's favor and goodness that God will prosper him and that he should prosper also in health and in soul. It was a wish from John to Gaius. This is reflected also in Paul's letter to Timothy in 1st Timothy 4:12. Let no man despise thy youth; but be thou an example of the believers, in word, in conversation, in charity, in spirit, in faith, and in purity. Show them by example and live godly. Imitate me, as Gaius imitated John. These are examples on how to be a child of God; how you ought to behave as a child of God. Paul showed such gratitude to the Philippians, Philippians 4:19, expressing his gratitude for their assistance and his wish that God will reward them.

People often use it as a prayer point and feel frustrated when such prayers are not answered accordingly. Can you live and show the same example as the Philippians had shown to Paul or as Gaius has shown to John the revelator? In Nehemiah 5:19 NIV, Nehemiah requested God to remember him with favor for all he has done for his people. His request for favor was based on what he has done for his people. Remember that this is a request and not a promise. I have prayed that prayer once and it worked for me, because I have helped my people on many fronts, and so have a genuine right to place a demand in line with God's words. This is the work of God. Believe on Him whom He has sent, John 6:29, 53, 56. The importance of Holy communion is included. The purpose and its significance is also highlighted.

All that is showing is that Jesus is God, and he used miracles which He Jesus performed to prove his case. Turning water to wine is a demonstration of a hand-over power and authority to his disciples because the miracles took place in their hands? Healing the nobleman's son by speaking the word is just to show us that the word of God is powerful and capable of changing and rearranging things. He fed 5000 men with a boy's lunch and the multiplication happened in the hands of the disciples. Jesus walked on water and even Peter walked a distance and defaulted. Jesus suspended the law of floatation to show that He can do it. He healed the man born blind to show that no matter the problems, God has the answer & solution, so that the works of God should be made manifest in him. Satan's effort to frustrate this man's life was instantly withered and disabled and so his life was set free.

He raised Lazarus from the dead to show He has power over death. Jesus proved His mission to silence or destroy the works of the devil with victory over this adversary of the human race, Colossians 2:14-15. Jesus was doing what the Father has sent Him to do, healing the unbelievers because of the mercy of God, healing the sinners because of God's grace, and healing those believing in Him based on Covenant. Jesus is the face of God as the Holy Spirit is the voice of God, the hand of God is the church. The Heart of God is His words, the heartbeat of God, His Authority. The promises of God are His extended hand. And He has given us the Power and the Authority to heal the sick and like Jesus said in Luke 4:18. The spirit of the Lord is upon me, because He has anointed me to preach the gospel (the good news) to the poor, he hath sent me to heal the broken-hearted, to preach deliverance to the captives and recovering of sight to the blind to set to liberty them that are bruised, and finally in verse 19 to preach, the acceptable year of the Lord. John is advising, saying in Chapter 15 the importance of our dependency on God and that without Him we are nothing, even though He has promised that He will never leave us or abandon us. He uses the vine tree to illustrate the issue.

Your faith like C.S. Lewis wrote "is the act of holding on to things your reason has once accepted, in spite of your changing moods" (Lewis 1980, 140). That was the operational definition of faith as confirmed by A.W. Tozer in his own book 'The pursuit of God.' When you accept Jesus as your savior God becomes the custodian of that covenant of faith and assumes full responsibility of your affair. As you continue to cooperate and collaborate with the conversion process, you will experience the type of conversion that C.S. Lewis went through which is described by his private secretary Walter Hooper, in his Discovery Series, C.S. Lewis, the story of a converted mind. Remember the patience of the old that gave results for Job, remember also Hebrew 10:36. "This spiritual conversion was not a single event. It was a process that transformed Lewis imagination, mind, conscience and expectation over a lifetime" (Lewis 2011, 3.) Your belief, your faith, is responsible for producing or generating the corresponding action. That is why it's said that faith without a corresponding action is dead. That action must be faith generated or belief generated. That action should be born out of your belief, faith or trust. The woman with the issue of blood was moved by what her faith in Christ generated and she could go against the traditions and defiled all protocols to touch Christ's garment. You are reminded again that God's power is voice activated.

The word of God must be considered at all times and what you fail to consider will harden your heart like Pharaoh of Egypt and like the disciples who forgot to consider the feeding of 5000 men when the storm showed up, as they were crossing over under Jesus command, Mark 6:52. Jesus has expected them to apply the principle of what they have been taught and seen demonstrated. Jesus had just finished showing how they ought to respond to issues like that. You discover your role in life through your relationship with others. The instructions you obey, is the future you create. Jesus must have asked them; can't you see how I fed the people with what we had and so why not use my name to still the storm? He expected them to use His name to perform. Jesus is happy when you use His name to be an answer to people's needs because it brings glory to the Father in heaven. If you can be an answer to the problems and questions of people, known and unknown to you, then Paul and John's wish are yours; Paul's wish to the Philippians, 4:19 and John's wish to Gaius, 3 John 2.

Chapter 13 deals with leadership, illustrating that Greatness is always measured by service, fellowship, while sin brings in darkness. Chapter 14 deals with answers beyond. Let not your hearts be troubled. Jesus promised them of a helper, another Comforter, which is the Holy spirit. The closing chapters deals with Jesus suffering death, burial and resurrection. Jesus voluntarily tasted death for us all, John 18:4. The disciples deserted Jesus in the hour of His greatest need. The brief time between Peters denial and the road to Golgotha was crowded with incidents. The trials, Peter's last denial, and the awful treatment suffered by Christ Jesus, and His last words are recorded in John 21. Jesus must erase the evidence of Peter's three times denial to save Peter from the consequences of denying Him before His Father. Jesus said since I have strengthened you Peter, strengthen my sheep. The Gospel of John opens with Christ in the bosom of His Father and closes with John in the bosom of Christ. Always remember to contact God first. What did God say about this issue? How was it handled by God and by Jesus on earth? Most of our response if any is for us to say, why not try praying, instead of telling the fellow to find what the bible is saying about it. How did the Bible settle similar issues and 'Why'? Consider God's words first before considering any other thing. John did a good job in showing us that Jesus was here to redeem us and position us for a better life. John 10:10, the thief cometh not but for to steal, and to kill and to destroy. I am come that they might have life and that they might have it more abundantly. The question is 'How' what has he come to steal, if not your joy, kill your desire and destroy your hope and expectations. If you know the How then you will be able to protect yourself and don't succumb by default. Thank you, John, for your exposition. Jesus greatest concern was to take us through the How, the laws of How and that is evangelism, we should start explaining the reasons why we must go through the process, using the Bible as our filter.

We must remember that Jesus was challenged to prove himself regarding his claims in chapter 6. Chapter 7:3-4 came up with the attack on the claims. Jesus even though they didn't understand that among other things he came to bring and sustain spiritual life instead of the physical life they were thinking about. Jesus did prove himself and threw the challenge back to his accusers, John 7:18, 10:38. Can we as Christians prove that we are what we claim to be? Can the court of justice for instance find us guilty of being a Christian by our actions, attitude and behavior? Haggai 1:5 wrote, it's time for us to consider our ways and like Malachi wrote, examine your ways. There are questions and there are scriptural promised answers for those who believe the What, How and Why of the Bible. Jesus was bold and courageous. Remember you cannot change what you cannot confront, John 7:25-26, 45-46.

PART FOUR

Jesus' Exit After the Cross and Paul's Arrival

Chapter 16
Paul's Call to Duty

The baton is handed over to the disciples to continue. Jesus has finished his assignment and gone back to the father and left the terrified and frightened disciples to carry on. They must wait to receive power as promised, Acts 1:8. Jesus must follow the same order of Moses whose laws came into serious effect after Moses death and God-given burial. We must remember that Adam failed God, his own chosen people of Israel failed Him. The prophets couldn't do much, and the law introduced, to teach and show them that they needed a Savior failed also. God must send his only begotten son to come and settle the debt we couldn't pay. Myer Pearlman remarks that "God's grace is revealed in His providing an atonement whereby He could both justify the ungodly and yet vindicate His holy, unchangeable law" (Pearlman 2007, 234). Dick Iverson with Bill Scheidler in their book Present Day Truths, said that, "the responsibilities given to the men of Israel in the Old Testament are to be fulfilled by the household of faith in the New Testament. Israel was a chosen nation by God to bless the world with the knowledge of true God and the messianic message. All Old testament foreshadowed what was to come to us in Christ. All the prophets spoke of Christ and His Body, the church" (Iverson and Scheidler 1976, 6).

We will all thank our Lord Jesus Christ, for making the sacrifice that has secured our freedom and eternal life, John 3:16, 36. We must learn what Jesus said and did, How He said it and did it and the why of it all, that's God's signature tune. To whom is Christ speaking to in this New testament, 1st Corinthians 10:32. There are three groups, the Jews, the Gentiles, and the Church of Christ. Like in the stories, the next question will be who will bail the cat. Who is going to start this crusade? Jesus has the answer; He has the plan. A zealous Roman Army Officer on a mission to Damascus to round up Christ followers and bring them to Jerusalem showed up. Jesus said this is the man with a mission. Acts 9, tells the whole story. Acts 3:22 confirmed it, and Acts 9:15, the Lord told Ananias to do what He has told him to do because Saul is now Christ chosen vessel to bear His name before the Gentiles and the Kings and the children of Israel. We have been given the power and authority to challenge devil and all things that have been holding us captive. Christ experience becomes our experience, John 15:7. The only entity in the entire universe that cannot be destroyed is the church, Mathew 16:18. There are laws governing the universe and some members of the church have been aiding and abetting Satan to scatter God's flock, the sheep of God.

It is no longer, you must do to become, as the law demands. It is now time to believe and receive as it is now by Grace and not by Law, John 1:17. It is now Galatians 5:4. What is the law saying? It's saying you must pay all the price, and Grace is saying it's all been paid for. Under the law you are servants working hard for your wages but under grace you are sons enjoying an inheritance, John 15:15-16. It's one body and you are part of that body. You must work for the body as part of the whole. Christ has said to Paul, you are the man to do this evangelism, to do this preaching and teaching to be an apostle and to prophesy Romans 1:5, NLT. "Through Christ God has given us the privilege and authority as apostle to tell the Gentiles everywhere what God has done for them, so that they will believe and obey him, bringing glory to His name", Ephesians 2:11-22. This is what my dissertation is saying, what God has said and done for the Gentiles, How He has said and Why He has said it, and His reason for doing it all. To bring the three groups to be one household of faith of God; the Jews, the Gentiles, and the Church of God. How did God do it?

He did it through His son Jesus Christ, so that whosoever believes in Him, will have an everlasting life, John 3:15. It pleased God that in Him should all fullness dwell, Colossians 1:19.

This goes to illustrate what Ephesians 2:8 says, for by grace are ye saved through faith and that not of yourself but it is the gift of God; Grace provides and faith takes. Faith only appropriates what grace has provided. Do we believe that God has through His grace made available all that we need to accomplish our goal? Do you believe that God has supplied scripturally promised answers to your questions and scriptural promised solutions to your problems? Romans 2:4 says that among other things that the goodness of God leadeth thee to repentance. God's goodness opens the door of repentance. Old testament was obedient to the Law. The New testament is obedient to the Grace and Truth. Master the signature tune of God, rightly understanding the what, the How and the Why of scripture. Taffi Dollar, wife of Dr. Creflo Dollar said in one of her sermons that some people have mouth but have no clue or idea how to use it. Many do not even know that the mouth is designed apparatus for partaking in the goodness of God. Psalms 23:6 says among other things that goodness and mercy will follow you all the days of your life. How? It is by you dwelling in the house of the Lord? Are you mission driven or position driven? Remember that even though obedience and faith are not very identical, one cannot operate without the other. God knows how to do it all, just trust Him, Jude 24, unto him that can keep you from falling and to present you faultless before the presence of his glory with exceeding joy. Our spiritual lives must be founded and governed by what God has said. What He has done, How He has said it and did it and why He said and did it. We must be aware that an example is not labelled a promise or vice versa.

The Holy Spirit guided Paul and his co-writers in writing what has become the church's doctrine for all time, though they little guessed they were writing for twenty centuries beyond as well as for their own day. The nine Christian church epistles and the four Pastoral and personal letters are of special importance to us in this present age. All scriptures, from Genesis to Revelation are written for us and is profitable to us, but not all scriptures are written about us or directly to us as members of the Body of Christ, as these thirteen epistles were. Therefore, if there is any part of the Bible which Christian believers should know thoroughly it is this part. Are you purpose driven as Rick Warren has said or are you mission driven, as many have written. Remember it is all what God has said, How He said and Why He said it, that matter. To understand it clearly, start with the Why, then climb up to the How and you will see that both are based on What God has said. That's the purpose for which you are created to do His will.

Chapter 17

Romans – The Christian Constitution

The book of Romans is regarded as the Constitution of Christianity. It explains doctrines most necessary for a correct knowledge and understanding of the Christian life. Issues like sin, salvation, justification, sanctification, predestination, the meaning of the cross, and the reason for the believers' love, faith, life and hope. This book deals with matters and answers questions of interest to believers. The book of Romans is like the believer's authority, a handbook like many Christians have written, and as practicing Christians, we should know what belongs to us. Our spiritual life begins when we are willing to allow God to be God in all aspects of our life. God has given us three levels of authority, per what my supervisor, Dr. Femi Falana taught us in class during my master's program. That the three levels of authority are Conscience, Bible, and Prayer. Prayer as C. Peter Wagner wrote in his book that "Christian prayer brings us into such intimacy with God that we are able to tune in to His love, grace, will, purpose and timing - and then adjust our own planning accordingly" (Wagner 1996, 24). This is how we ought to do things in God's way.

Every movement of revival in the history of the Christian Church has related to the teachings found in Romans. Paul in Romans 1:16 said that "he is not ashamed of the gospel of Christ for it is the power of God unto salvation to everyone that believeth, to the Jews first and also to the Greek". Once you receive or accept Jesus as your Savior, God takes over. You now change how you see the Bible. You now see the Bible as a Will, Hebrews 9:15-17. A Will goes into effect after the death of the person, so see yourself in God's Will. Everything that Christ has done is credited to your account, just as if we had done it. You are immediately declared righteous. We have His righteousness and as such we are justified. We are made just by believing on Christ's finished work and not by our own works. The just shall live by faith, and that is, you live by believing. It's your faith in believing and not in doing which is self-performance. The book of Romans shows us the 'Hows' of achieving our goals and arriving at our destiny as our believing generates, the corresponding actions required. So always turn to your believer's manual, God's signature tune.

All is about What we ought to say and do, How we ought to say and do it. Why we ought to say it and reason it out through the Bible, Hebrew 4:1-2. James is telling us what to say, James 4:15 and the assurance of God in 2nd Peter 3:9. The How always settles the issues of what and why all the time. Paul is telling us that not only the Israelites have a promised land, we Gentiles now have all the promises of God to be ours, based on what Jesus Christ has done for us. Since God doesn't change these promises given through His anointed leaders and prophets in Old testament still stand, Deuteronomy 6:10-13, Joshua 24:13. Even Isaiah prophesied that even at old age that our labor will not be in vain, Isaiah 65:21-24, 1st Corinthians 2:9, as well as 2nd Corinthians 1:20-22. These are covenant promises which can never be withdrawn or cancelled, Psalms 89:34. The question to ask yourself is this, how did I get here? If where you are is good, then let the best get better, but if not, ask, seek and knock to know How to get out and be relocated and repositioned as Rahab was positioned to be an answer to Israel spies, Joshua 2:12-21. Our problem is that we have left being what we are created to be and like the book of Anglican (Protestant) common prayer stated in its revised edition, and I quote, "Almighty and most merciful Father; We have erred, and strayed from thy ways like lost sheep. We have followed too much the devices and desires of our own hearts. We have offended against thy holy laws. We have left undone those things which we ought to have done; and we have done those things which we ought not to have done; and there is no health in us", this is where most of us are today. We have left the human beings to become the human I, and like Lucifer in Isaiah 14:12-14 who lost it all. We want to perform to become. Which foundation are we operating from? Paul is advising us to labor to enter into the rest and stop carrying the burden of pride and its attachments, Proverbs 13:10.

In Romans 10:14-17, Paul succinctly exposed the importance of knowing how Jesus spiritually, emotionally and scripturally, connected us to how to apply the biblical principles of 'How' to our daily needs as shown in Ephesians 1:15-17-21. Paul also showed us how to scripturally pray God's will, and in Luke 17:7-8-10. Luke explains how we can use our God given faith as a servant to appropriate what grace has made available, Ephesians 2:8. How to put your faith to work. In Philippians 2:12, Paul again showed us, 'How' to work out our salvation, how to acknowledge what is within us, Philemon 6. Remember again that life is not what you expect but what you permit. Make formed decision based on what God said, How He said it and why He said it. Like Rick Warren commented in his book, 'The Purpose Driven', knowing God's purpose for creating you will reduce your stress, focus your energy, simplify your decisions, give meaning to your life and most importantly, prepare you for eternity (Warren 2002, 30-33). The relevant issue about your relationship with God is changing from what we do to what we ought to do, to bring glory to Him.

Romans 12 – 15 deals with the 'What', the 'How' and the 'Why', we call reasonable service. God had in Romans 1:19-20 revealed himself through the things we see having endowed us with the intuitive knowledge of Him and the spiritual instinct, that we have no reasons for excuse.

(1) Our responsibility as believers towards God is found in Romans

12:1-2. God's will are two, the permissible will of God and the perfect will of God.

(2) Our relationship towards fellow believers and other people Romans 12:3-16 and then 12:17-21 respectively. Recompense to no man evil for evil.

(3) Our responsibility towards government, Romans 13:1-7.

(4) The law of love as seen in daily living, Romans 13:8 – 15:3.

(5) Jews and Gentile are supposed to be one in Christ, Romans 15:4-13, Ephesians 2:11-22.

Paul greeted his friends with a show of gratitude in Romans 16. General advice. You are reminded not to judge others unless you base it on the word of God, Romans 2:1-4. The society will only be transformed by men and women shaped by love and the fear of the Lord, Proverbs 8:13. In Romans 12:2. We are advised not to conform to this world but be transformed by the renewing of our mind that we may prove what is that good and acceptable and perfect will of God.

No one can claim to be serving God if you are not doing His will. Your service to God must be based on His will and not yours. When you serve people with the gift God has given you then you are in the will of God. It's only when you are working with God in His will, will you be able to serve God in spirit and in truth, John 4:24. You can't do this if you are not working in the will of God. Goodness and mercy of Psalms 23:6 will not follow you if you are not in the will of the Father. When you read, what is said in Ephesians 2:8. For by grace are you saved through faith and that not of yourself. It is the gift of God. It's a gift you didn't work for. You often hear preachers shouting on top of their voices that your faith moves God. How can what God has given you, as a gift, move Him when you use it for God's purpose? Faith is simply for appropriating what Grace has provided. Its practical express of your confidence in Him, taking Him at His word. We don't need to brag about it, noting that all these good things are from God. 1st Corinthians 4:7, and this takes me to examine what Paul is telling the people of Corinth at this stage. Paul in dealing with the nine Christian church epistles, that is from Romans through Thessalonians, revealed to us How God works using people, circumstances and events to reach out to His creation. Paul's letters showed his concerns and the attempts and compassion he expressed towards the church and the congregation.

Paul is showing proof of his statement, evidence, 1st Thessalonians 5:21. As stated by Dr. J. Sidlow Baxter, "Yes the Jesus of the New testament is the fulfillment of Old testament ceremony, history, philosophy, prophecy. In the Old testament, He is coming. In the Gospels, He has come in visible humanity. In the Epistles, He has come in by the invisible Holy Spirit. In the Apocalypse, He comes back in the glory of World Empire. The fulfillments at His first coming prove Old testament prophecy to be Divine; and they equally guarantee that the still unfulfilled remainder, in both Old testament and New testaments will just as certainly burst into occurrence when the predestined hour strikes" (Baxter 1996, 97 'New Testament and Old Section').

How do we remember our loved ones, both living and the departed? How? By the help of the Holy Spirit, our comforter, John 14:26. Knowing Jesus is the answer and receiving Him as your Savior sets you on course, John 14:16. The divine indwelling of the Holy Spirit is conditional on love and your willingness to obey Jesus words, what He said, How He said it and why He said it. This is the New testament anthem, and this is God's scriptural signature tune, 'Knowing you Jesus' by Graham Kendrick.

Chapter 18
Paul's Epistles

1st Corinthians. The question is why was Paul writing the believers in Corinth. His aim in this epistle is to bring the Corinthians actions and lifestyle into closer harmony with God's will and expectation. Paul found it necessary based on reports he received (household of Chloe and others chapter 1-6) to rebuke the believers for their division, for condoning immorality, for their lawsuits, with one another, for their abuse of the Lord's Supper, and for disorderliness in the church. They should understand the purpose and the significance of the holy communion. This letter makes positional sanctification practical. In chapter 1:1-31, Paul dealt with our Lord's willingness, faithfulness and oneness of mind, purpose and judgement. Paul's purpose was to show them the reality of Romans 1:16, stressing that Christ's redemptive work opened the way for God to extend His grace to sinful man to pour out upon him such benefit as wisdom, righteousness and sanctification. Paul's advice and correction centered on our need to have shared spiritual stimulation of fellow believers. We need to demonstrate a worshipping heart, a willing heart, to stimulate and energize others while being stimulated to love and do good works. Through this we can spiritually identify God's provisions.

Scripture and experience do tell us that Human wisdom will always tell you to get all you can and can all you get. Human nature advices us to believe only what you can see, with your five-sensory mechanism. God's wisdom advices us to, give as we can and believe what we cannot see, which is more real to the believers. Enjoy service and expect persecution. It advices that your life is expected to reflect a difference. Spiritual success does require commitment to others, as Nathan brought it up to David in 1st Chronicles Chapter 17. Paul in this section chapters 1-6 showed that spiritual gifts do not insure spirituality of believers. He talked about natural man, spiritual man and carnal mind. How to settle disputes was mostly hammered home. The quarrel of who planted and who watered illustration of Chapter 3:3-6 of 1st Corinthians, was settled. Correct understanding on how the kingdom of God works, showing that its God who gives the increase, Paul provided the word/seed, Apollos provided the faith/ watering.

Marriage issues regarding responsibilities of both husbands and wives were addressed because Paul foresaw by spirit the persecution that was coming. One of the reasons as stated on the footnotes why God told Moses to record the experiences of the children of Israel was that He had Paul and the Corinthians believers in mind. Chapter 12 deals with spiritual gifts, pointing to unity, oneness that is needed especially in the church. Love is the strongest force on earth. You can give without loving but you cannot love without giving. All things are valueless without love, 1st Corinthians 13 is all about love. Love, faith and hope, are correlated to the Holy Trinity, God the Father, the Son and the Holy Spirit.

Love is regarded as the strongest force in the universe. It brings things together and Hebrew 1:3 said it all. That Love is the word of His power which is responsible for holding all things together. Holding families together, friendships together, countries together. I agree with Charles Haanel's statement in Rhonda Byrne's book, The Secret, that "there is no greater power in the universe than the power of Love, the power of attraction". In fact, some of the greater thinkers of the past referred to the law of attraction as the law of Love. Romans 12:9 let love be without dissimulation. 'Abhor that which is evil, cleave to that which is good. The love is to be genuine and unfeigned'.

"The utter necessity of love, the moral excellency of love and the abiding supremacy of love are all noted", 1st Corinthians 13:1- 13. Chapter 14 talks on prophecy, its purpose and significance.

Chapter 15 deals with Christ resurrection and its importance as a distinguishing factor for believers and nonbelievers. Chapter 16 shows the importance of planning. In conclusion of this section, Paul was addressing his commitment to spreading the gospel and that his top priority was enabling others to understand it. Stressing the reality of the gospel of Christ he believed even though God has given us numerous blessings and rights we should be willing to give them up if it would help someone to know Christ. The example of Martha, Mary and their brother Lazarus shows us that God sees all that we do. Our service to others as Martha who takes time to serve, like Mary who takes time to worship and finally like Lazarus who testifies. Each of us has our place at the table. What are you bringing to the table? God honors our conviction and testimony that will encourage and influence others. Spiritual gifts glorify God and build up the body of Christ. Gifts should never be misused, envied or cause division.

2nd Corinthians. Of all of Paul's epistles 2nd Corinthians is the most personal. Paul was compelled to write at this point to vindicate himself. The presence of false teachers at Corinth who were questioning his authority, impugning his motives, undermining his authority, had made it necessary for Paul to defend himself and the ministry. In making this defense, he was compelled to relate experience about which he would rather have been silent. Why was Paul so challenged physically and otherwise? Probably he was enforcing his opinion on mankind. Paul here showed how to handle unfair treatment like John Bevere mentioned in his book, 'Undercover'. So, Paul goes out to show how to handle such issues when they show up. Taken from 2nd Corinthians 2:9 Paul was testing whether they were going to be obedient to completion. Whether they could respect the delegated authority from God. How Paul handled this issue when compared with his statement on 2nd Corinthians 11:29 doesn't fit in as regards complete dependent on God as expressed by John Bevere using 1st Peter 2:13, 19, 21. Considering 1st Peter 5:7 and 2nd Corinthians 11:29, Paul may have by default missed the mark somehow, but who knows? John Bevere is saying in verse 19 "that God is pleased with you when, for the sake of conscience, you patiently endure unfair treatment" (Bevere 2011, 162). What is our calling folk, John asks? To handle unfair treatment correctly. Jesus gave us His personal example. What good does handling or suffering unfair treatment accomplish, when handling it correctly. John Bevere answers: "(1) It makes room for God's righteous judgement. (2) It develops the character of Christ. (3) Our submission under this treatment glorifies God." (Bevere 2011, 162).

As popularly said, there is no saint without a past and no sinner without a future. Paul's missionary principles and practice of the apostle Paul Chapter 1-7 Christian Stewardship is covered by Chapters 8-9 and finally his vindication of his apostleship and ministry is covered by Chapters 10-13. Paul's advice was that those who minister in Christ's name must be honest and have good reputation among believers and nonbelievers. We know it's not easy to fix our eyes on what is unseen, but it is necessary, 2nd Corinthians 4:18. Paul is encouraging every believer not to undermine his or her gifts and talents instructing that they look in at Hebrew 11, hall of faith and see how God and the people of the ancient maneuvered issues because of God-given faith. He cited that David's track record left little to be desired but his repentant spirit was unquestionable therefore labelling him man after God's heart. What we may lack in perfection, God makes up in love so the scriptures say.

Galatians. There are four evangelical epistles, Romans, 1 & 2 Corinthians, and Galatians. We have the doctrine in Romans, reproof in 1 & 2 Corinthians and thorough correction of wrong doctrine in

Galatia. You read Romans, (regarded as Christian constitution) to be well grounded in Christian doctrine, Corinthians to be guided in Christian practice, and Galatians to be on guard against deceptive errors. The Hows and Whys of the Bible is highly highlighted in Galatian epistle of Paul. The question has always been, why do Paul write these letters? Why should Paul take some risks which are obvious to attract criticisms, attacks and challenges? When you look at what Paul wrote in 1st Corinthians 9:17, you will immediately see why he responds to the letters and inquiries from his converts. His goal is to prevent the readers from embracing a false gospel and to encourage them to retain their spiritual freedom in Christ, Gal 5:1.

(1) Looking at it globally the Gospel of Christ was being perverted by Judaizers who were discrediting Paul's apostleship and message. Paul was vehemently exposing their sin and they assumed they had every reason and right to challenge his opinion on certain issues.

(2) The Galatians were by default dropping off from the doctrine of Salvation by divine grace through faith in Christ. Ephesians 2:8,

(a) This was seeking a way to be justified by the law using the Old testament demands to meet New testament requirement. Law vs Grace.

(b) Instituting the observance of days and months and seasons and years and

(c) Supplementing the work of the Holy Spirit by works of the flesh which is a circumcision issue. Dr. James L. Snyder who edited A.W. Tozer's book on Alive in the Spirit, said that "the authority of the Holy Spirit must begin with the individual Christian and then flow over into the local congregation"

(Tozer 2016, 7). According to Tozer, "one of the things that has replaced the work of the Holy Spirit in the local church is entertainment" (Tozer 2016, 9). He is of the opinion "that worship and entertainment are opposites and cannot be mixed. It is either one or the other" (Tozer 2016, 10). Only the Holy spirit can do the work of God. It begins with the Holy Spirit and end with the Holy Spirit" (Tozer 2016, 10).

(3) Paul was calling the Galatians back from the law of Moses, to grace, from legalism to faith, to salvation by faith apart from works.

We must take note that Justification and Sanctification are not achieved by works of the law but by faith. It's a process which takes some time and is lifelong process. Paul maintained that his apostleship and message came by revelation of the risen Christ, Acts 9:1-19. Paul explained that the Mosaic Law do not stand in opposition to the Abrahamic covenant, for it was never intended to save man. It was given to educate man to his need for salvation by faith. The law is being used as a teacher, school master. Chapters 5 – 6 shows the How and Whys of the Bible as written down in the epistles. To point out that Christian liberty does not mean that you have been given a license to sin. Paul teaches that a Christian should live by the power of the Holy Spirit and that when he does, it manifests in his life not the works of the flesh but the fruit of the spirit, Galatians 5:22-23. The fruit of the flesh is Galatians 5:19-21. Paul gave points on How and Why we should adhere to the scriptural promised answers and solutions.

(a) You are to hold fast to the liberty of grace since the law cannot save you.

(b) Turn away from false teachers who have perverted the gospel and made you slaves to legalism.

(c) Though free from mosaic law, you are not free to sin.

Let a prayer for strength be a reflex reaction to temptation. Resist the devil and he will flee from you. How? When we submit ourselves before God, be mindful to support your ministers and you will thereby reap the divine blessing. Beware of the Judaizers. In conclusion, Paul is telling the believers in Galatia that they cannot know the will of God for their lives without acknowledging the purpose and significance of Christ sacrifice and what it stands for. The Judaizers thought that the Gentile believers had to obey Jewish laws, in order to be saved but Paul corrected that false teaching. Paul's letter assured us of God's faithfulness to His promises and showed us the power of love in chapter 5:6. For in Jesus Christ neither circumcision availeth anything nor uncircumcision, but faith which worketh by love. You must be in the will of God to serve God willingly and become thoroughly converted. Knowing that you are no longer servants but friends to Jesus Christ, John 15:15-17, confirms and establishes you as a child of God.

Ephesians. The epistles of Paul to the Ephesians, Colossians, Philippians, and to Philemon, are collectively called the prison Epistles, because they were written during Paul's first Roman imprisonment. It is here that God's signature tune is fully demonstrated. Some have called this epistle the action plan of God. What God said and did. How he said it and did it and why He said and did it. It also showed how God designed us and why we are so designed;

(1) to learn the truth of the What, the How, and the Why of the Bible.

(2) to inquire, so as to ask, seek and knock.

(3) to wonder how and why God has created us.

Let us rejoice for this is the day the Lord had made with scripturally promised answers and solutions to our concerns. Study to know the what, the How and the Why and give God thanks for His goodness, praise for His greatness, and worship Him for His holiness. Jesus has made the Jewish and Gentile believers into one new man as Chapter 2:15 said. When you look at Chapter 2, you will see how He made it through relationship. The old relationship chapter 2:11-12 and New relationship Ephesians 2:13-22. Remember and don't forget what he said in chapters 2:8. Remember Paul's statement that the believer may know the love of Christ which passeth all knowledge, the revelation of the mystery that the Gentiles should be, fellow heirs of the body of Christ and partakers of the promise in Christ by the gospel. How did God set out the plan? The plan is given to the church through the ministry gifts of the apostles, prophets, evangelists, pastors and teachers, and from there the plan goes into the rest of the body of Christ. The first big 'How' is found in chapter 4:23. And be renewed in the spirit of your mind after your born-again experience. Why? See the why in Romans 8:19, for the earnest expectation of the creature waiteth for the manifestation of the sons of God. Look at your new life in Christ as seen in 2nd Corinthians 5:17, "If any man be in Christ, he is a new creature, old things are passed away, behold all things are new". This is the touch of redemption and as Oswald Chambers put it, the inner reality of redemption is that it creates all the time as earlier mentioned.

In Colossians 1:19, for it pleased the father that in him should all fullness dwell. How is this done? You see it in Ephesians 6:10-18, demonstrating how it is done. It involves putting on the whole armor of God, taking note of

(1) the Belt of Truth

(2) the Breastplate of righteousness

(3) the Shoes of peace

(4) the Shield of faith

(5) the Helmet of Salvation

(6) the Sword of the Spirit. This is how you defeat your enemies and become the overcomer and a partaker of the promises of Christ.

The Epistles of Philippians is Epistle of joy. There has grown up between Paul and the Philippian church a bond of friendship closer than that which existed between Him and any other church. It was Paul's priced bust of self-sufficiency and that it was only from the Philippians that Paul agreed to accept a gift, see Phil 4:10-20. Why did Paul accept gifts from them? Paul must have seen and observed their willingness to support his assignment. His using the word 'joy', almost sixteen times and showing that there is joy in the sacrificial giving of oneself (2:17,18) and of one's goods (4:18) to meet the needs of others and to do God's will thus following Jesus example (2:4-11). This is the joy that conquers all odds, and that is what our Bishop Harry Jackson of Hope Christian Church of Beltsville Maryland calls it. Paul was expressing his gratitude to the saints in Philippians. Since I heard it from Billy Graham that ingratitude is a sin, I have always expressed my gratitude to those who have helped me. Look at the benefit a leper got out of the ten that showed up. It earned him a complete healing which is wholeness, meaning nothing missing and nothing broken. Paul is showing the importance of Christian joy, stressing that

(1) there is joy in suffering for through that God accomplishes good, 1:12-14.

(2) there is joy in knowing Christ and experiencing His resurrection

power (3:8-10).

There is joy when harmony prevails among the brethren (2:4, 4:2-5). There is joy over the adequacy of Christ (4:13-19) which produces contentment for every circumstance of life. His letter points to the joy in Christ, and our true goal should be to know Christ and his power.

In Colossian, epistle Paul emphasizes Christ as the head of the Church which is His body. Fullness in Christ, power and joy are acknowledged. It has always been why did Paul write the letters? What do we learn from these letters? It's all about understanding how we can apply it in our lives and be able to sort out our problems. When we go to church we want to hear what the preacher is preaching, his explanations, how he or she is explaining it and why he or she is doing it that way. How can we apply it to make course corrections and adjustments needed in our lives? That's what theology is all about. Some of the contributions of writers are recognized. Writers like Roger E Olson in his book the Story of Christian theology, Gregg R Allison in his book, Historical theology, Dr. J. Sidlow Baxter in his book, Explore the book and Prof. Millard J Erickson in his 2nd and 3rd edition of Christian theology. These are good books recommended by Newburgh Theological Seminary. All these books in one way or the other demonstrate the signature tune of God.

It's now knowing Jesus the author and finisher of our faith. It's now a question of what do you do with what you hear and what you know. How do you process issues of concern? Are you ready to handle the process before asking for the promise? Remember like T.D. Jakes said in one of his TV sermon, that there is a gap between you and the seat, you are aiming at, a seat you want to occupy, there's a cup to be dealt with. Gnostic bewitchers at Colossae were insinuating that their own new inner knowledge be acknowledged in the Gospel. They denied the fully deity and true humanity of the Lord Jesus Christ. Paul rebuked them for that error. It is still around some denomination who think that Jesus didn't do enough and so retain penance in their sacrament. The pre-eminence of Christ is noted. He is first in nature, first in the church, first in resurrection, ascension and glorification. He is the only mediator, savior and source of life, Hebrew 7:25. That's why Paul confirmed and established this fact in chapter 2:14-15, Colossian 1:16,19. When you read and understand these verses and what they stand for, your scriptural promised answers and promised solutions, will stand out clearly. The question, who is a disciple? Know who you are in Christ. Know your enemy and how to go about dealing with them. Knowing the weapon of your warfare, will be clearer. Remember and forget not that God's power is voice activated. Use it if you believe it. It belongs to you. Paul is reminding us in what Peter wrote in 2nd Peter 1:8, "for if these things be in you, and abound, they make you, that ye shall neither be barren nor unfruitful in the knowledge of our Lord Jesus Christ".

The Thessalonian letters. Paul's letters constitute questions asked and answers returned, Problems raised and solutions tendered, leaving us to study and listen to God's scriptural signature tune. It's all about rightly understanding the what, How and Why of the Bible. What was the issues raised by the people of Thessalonica (Salonika today) concerning all the fundamentals of faith, including 2nd coming of Christ, in relation to the believers, encouragement, comfort, watchfulness and sanctification?

(1) Timothy reported to Paul that some believers were concerned that their dear ones who had died in Christ would have no part in the glory of His return.

(2) Other believers were thinking that Christ's return was imminent and had to cease working. So, Paul was lovingly correcting the

faulty thinking of the Thessalonians.

The two areas of concern here is 1st Thessalonians 5:17, which deals with pray without ceasing and verse 18, which says in everything give thanks, for this is the will of God in Christ Jesus concerning you. This goes to prove the fact that when you see 'All' it concerns God and when you come across, 'Every' it concerns us biblically you and I. God is God of All in All. "The only time Christians have the unlimited power of the Holy spirit at their disposal is when they are obedient to the will of God" (Lahaye 1999, 62). So, all in all our prayers should be to acknowledge our complete dependence upon God as our source, in all areas of our life, Philemon 6. We must remember that without regeneration, we end up being "Christian by assumption, by manipulation or instruction rather than by regeneration" (Lahaye 1999, 120). This is what A.W Tozer wrote in his book, 'Experiencing the presence of God'; "What is of God uses implantation of a new nature within the heart of a person, causing him instinctively to live like a Christian. Causing him to naturally follow after righteousness and true holiness" (Tozer 2010, 120). I agree with him completely in that we must live doing what we ought to do to please God, and thinking on those important things as stated in Philippians 4:8.

In the 1st epistle to Thessalonians we have the day of Christ, in the second epistle, we have the day of the Lord (judgement). Paul was the first to teach on the rapture or Christ's return for His church. Between the two aspects or stages of the second Advent there is the period known as the Great tribulation.

Paul's letter corrects misapprehension that has arisen over Paul's first epistle. In the first epistle, Paul told them to wait while working, in 2nd Thessalonians. Paul told them to work while waiting. There are promises of Christ's second coming, especially to those who are expecting Him. And those who are going through the trials of their faith. These are for information and necessary action. We should close our ears to the manifold voices of compromise and perch ourselves on the branch of truth. Listen to God's signature tune, on a daily basis. For those who live for this world, that's bad news. But for those who live for the world to come, it's an encouraging promise. Recognize that your hope is based on what God has done for you in Christ. Christ in you the hope of glory, Colossians 1:27. Remember and forget not Deuteronomy 9:7. The what, the How and the Why of God which was completely revealed by Jesus in the New testament. Consider it as Abraham did, in Romans 4:19. That is the goal of my dissertation, to bring everything to focus. To connect all the needed connections, all the dots and present one front at an eye level. Paul's foreknowledge of the situation helped him to advice Timothy accordingly, 1st Timothy 4:12.

Chapter 19
Hebrew's through to Jude

The 1st and 2nd Chapters of Timothy along with the book of Titus are regarded as the pastoral epistles, as they are taken up with the Christian Ministry and church government. These three epistles, addressed to individuals and not to congregation has as their central theme, effectiveness in the Christian Ministry with emphasis on the reading of the scriptures, exhortation and teaching.

There is a distinction between 1st Timothy and 2nd Timothy, in the first we have the ideal church every pastor ought to have, and in the 2nd, the ideal pastor every church ought to have. Whenever ordained ministers lose contact with the congregation, they cease to be effective tool in the hand of God. What Paul knew pushed him to write Timothy. Paul was aware of his approaching martyrdom, foresaw the coming apostasy and false teachers and was encouraging Timothy in his position as Bishop at Ephesus on what to do. The what, the How and the Why are now up as always. Christ is presented as the Mediator between God and Man, 1st Timothy 2:5, Hebrew 7:25. Christ is the Savior of all who believe, 1st Timothy 4:10. What was Paul's advice to Timothy's problem with his congregation? Paul told Timothy how to solve that problem.

Paul concluded his writing by a final charge to Timothy, 1st Timothy 6:20. That as a young bishop he should be able to fulfill his duties considering God's authority. Can also keep that which has been committed to his trust, avoiding profane and vain bubbling and oppositions of science falsely so called. Remember that the love of God and the fear of the Lord is nothing but recognizing God's authority, respecting God's authority and responding to God's authority. "For there is one God and Father from whom are all things and one Lord

Jesus Christ through whom are all things, and one Holy spirit, in whom are all things" (Bettensen and Maunder 1999, 100).

This is what Oswald Chambers, also author of My Utmost for His Highest, wrote in his studies of the sermon on the mount, "at the bar of common sense, Jesus Christ's statements are those of a fool, but bring them to the bar of faith and the word of God, and you begin to find with awestruck spirit they are the words of God" (Chambers 1992, 71). I do believe that both reason and faith do play their parts in scriptures, and Jesus is teaching us how to apply each to achieve our goal. As I am concluding, I must recall that this statement is collaborated by Robert Louis Wilken's book (Wilken 2003, 163).

2nd Timothy represents Paul's last will and testament which is often a treasure. Paul's advice is that he should continue to press on and obey to completion. He must demonstrate loyalty to the God-given mission and to the teaching and preaching in line with the word of God, chapter 4:6-8. Paul writes his own epitaph. What sayest thou? The old preacher exhorts the young evangelist to stir up the gift that is in him and the old soldier reminds his successor that he has fought a good fight and has kept the faith, 2nd Timothy 4:7. The Bible here gives advice to the spiritual man, 2nd Timothy 2:15, study to shew thyself approved unto God, a workman that needeth not to be ashamed, rightly dividing the word of truth. This is what God is telling the spiritual man. To the Theologians, John 13:17, "if ye know these things, happy are ye if ye do them". This is recorded by Myer Pearlman in his book, Knowing the doctrine of the Bible, page 8. "It takes all the Bible to make the whole Bible" (Tozer 2016, 9) wrote Dr. James L. Snyder, who compiled and edited A.W. Tozer's book on Alive in the Spirit, in his introductory pages. Paul in Acts 20:27, declared that "for I have not shunned to declare unto you all the counsel of God". The epistle to Titus compares with first epistle to Timothy, written about the same time to friends of the apostle, who had responsibility of pastoral oversight. Titus emphasizes the godly conduct of all believers. He served Paul as a special apostolic delegate to Corinth. The three pastoral epistles are a Trinity in unity, exhorting us to guard the precious deposit of the Gospel. In first Timothy, it protects it, in 2nd Timothy it proclaims it and here in Titus, it practices it. While there is a charge and a challenge in Timothy respectively, in Titus there is a caution that sound faith must be accompanied by good works. Faith causes us to be what the law truly wants, Roman 3:31. Good works signify our gratitude to God. The key passage of this letter, chapter 2:11-15 is a constant reminder of what God has done for us in making us His children. The purpose and significance of these verses should not be ignored along with its write-up on qualifications and code of conduct for the clergy. David in Psalms 55:22 shows us the power of How. As he processed his feeling, he discovered the How or found a way to rest in his troubled thoughts, which brings us to the NT verse in 1st Peter 5:7. Casting all your cares upon him, for he careth for you. Jesus promised the apostles that the Holy spirit will bring all things to their remembrance What Jesus said and did, How he said and did it all and Why. They were to remember the works and words of Jesus when writing the New testament, John 14:26. The Holy spirit will make it possible.

The Epistle to Philemon. Paul centers around a runaway slave, Onesimus, whose Master was Philemon, a Christian convert of Paul. This epistle taken as a polite one, affords us a view of the Apostle's courtesy, prudence and skillful address. Its chief value lies in picture it gives us of the practical outworking of Christian doctrine in everyday life and of the relation of Christian to social problem as at that time. The power of the gospel in the solution of social problems is demonstrated. Here again it depended on what Paul said and did. How he said it and did it and why he said and did it all. How did Paul handle the issue? There is a scriptural promised answers and solutions to our everyday issues. Onesimus is a runaway slave, who made his way to Rome where he met Paul and was converted. Paul may have either been told or realized that Onesimus was a runaway slave but finding him a sincere convert and devoted friend decided to intervene on his behalf. Although Onesimus had repented of his sin, there was a call for restitution which could be made only by the slave's returning and submitting himself to his master. Even though this was a sacrifice for Paul, it was a much greater one, for Onesimus. The sense of right required Paul to return the slave but the constraint of love caused him to intercede for him and save him from punishment. Paul simply identified himself with Onesimus. This is God-like action.

How did Paul start? He writes Philemon with a salute asking about the family, commends him for his love, faith, and hospitality. Paul reminds Philemon that he is indebted to him for his salvation and expresses his confidence that Philemon will obey and even do more than Paul has asked, vs 19-22. This epistle presents the relation of Christianity to slavery and teaches principles that undermine and overthrow wrong systems. Why did Paul take these steps to save and deliver Onesimus who could have been mocked, scourged, mutilated, crucified, or even thrown to the wild beasts? Why did Christianity not attempt to overthrow this system?

(1) To have done so would have required a tremendous revolution.

(2) The religion of Christ reforms by love, not by force.

We are reminded that in Christ all social distinctions are removed, Galatians 3:28, Phil 6. This is high powered letter to Philemon. Even though he has every right to be angry for Onesimus who stole from him and ran away to Roman, yet Paul was seeking that Philemon not to free him from slavery but free him from anger. He was pleading with Philemon to tamper mercy with justice since this was not a normal circumstance. Paul explains that Onesimus fled as a slave, but returns as a believer. Acknowledge who you are in Christ. The love God expects from us goes beyond the standard of this world. Love, the force of the law of attraction has been regarded as the greatest power; use it if you believe it. Remember that forgiveness is necessary and as Gary Inrig wrote "forgiveness doesn't mean forgetting to remember but remembering to forget" (Inrig 2005, 124).

Hebrews. The Hebrew epistle whose author remains unknown has a great message and precious truths that are revealed to us, about our Lord's heavenly priesthood and superiority. Christ is the new and living way. Every line was designed for the instruction and admonition of those who were Hebrew in blood and Christian in faith, many of whom were in danger of going back to Judaism. The first believers on Him were Jews and Gospel itself is to the Jews first. The book shows the Hebrew Christians and to all of us the superiority of the Lord Jesus Christ over Judaism, 1-4. The religion of Jesus Christ is superior to Judaism, for it has a better covenant, a better high priest, a better sacrifice and a better tabernacle. The writer of Hebrews did a fine job, dividing the epistle into four sections. The first section deals with superiority of the person of Christ Chapter 1:4 - 4:13. The second section deals with superiority of the priesthood of Christ, Chapter 4:14 – 10:18. Third section. Exhortation of faith, hope and love, chapter 10:19 – 13:19. The fourth, conclusion. Here we find what God said and did concerning both the Jews and the Gentiles, with all these scripturally heart shaping promises. God had to confirm and establish what He said and did, the promises He made. For when He made promise to Abraham (6:13) because he could swear by no greater, he swore by himself. Verse 16 is an oat for confirmation ending all strife. Embracing salvation involves acknowledging redemption, Hebrew 9:12,15. Christ work is completed. How?

(a) He is the fulfiller of all the major offering in the book of Leviticus

(b) He is our advocate and our forerunner.

(c) He stands before God now representing us as our intercessor.

The question should now be, how can we locate the answers to my questions? How can I locate the solutions to my problems? What is the Bible saying? What are the preachers preaching? It is all about what God said and did, how He said it and did it, and why; That's the theology. This is God's scriptural signature tune, and it pleased God, the Father that in Christ should all fullness dwell, Colossians 1:19. He said in Hebrew 10:35-36, "Cast not your confidence, which hath great recompense of reward. For you have need of patience, that after you have done the will of God, ye might receive the promise". What are you being advised to do? To hold fast to the profession of your hope without wavering. Why? Because he that promised is faithful. Therefore 1st Corinthians 4:7 showed up to ask you the question. "For who maketh thee to differ from another? And what hast thou that thou didst not receive? Now if thou didst receive it, why dost thou glory, as if thou hadst not received it?". Faith is another area strengthen up with Abraham as the father of faith. He showed it in Romans 4:19-21. What did Abraham do? He hoped against hope, "not weak in faith, he considered not his own body now dead and he did not stagger at the promise of God through the unbelief. He was strong in faith giving glory to God and being fully persuaded that what He had promised, He was able also to perform". This is showing us that whatever God's word you fail to consider, whatever miracles of God you fail to consider and acknowledge, you develop a hardened heart, Mark 6:52. In Hebrews chapter 12:1, he shows you how to run your own race. How to overcome your everyday issue in your life. Why do you trust the word of God? Why trust God? Hebrews 13:8 tells you why. Jesus Christ who is the author and finisher of our faith is the same, yesterday, and today and forever. So, do something that demonstrates faith.

All the Christian books I have read are all talking on the same God's signature tune. The what, the How and the why. We are bringing it to focus; So, the most important thing is knowing this. Jesus who is our all, our best, our joy and our righteousness and this forms the anthem of the New Testament. Like the popular church song goes, knowing you Jesus by Graham Kendrick; 'Knowing you Jesus, knowing you, there is no greater thing. You're my all, you're the best you're my joy, my righteousness, and I love you Lord'. This is what Paul was saying in Philippians 3:10-11, to know Christ, to experience His power, the resurrection power, sharing in His suffering, being made like Jesus at death, experiencing the resurrection from dead. This reminds you of John 15:7 which says, "If you abide in me, and my words abide in you, ye shall ask what ye will, and it shall be done unto you". The key is your knowing Jesus, your knowing Him, personally and experientially.

Chapter 20

Revelation and Review of Paul's Stewardship

The book of James is the most practical of all epistles. Noted for its efficiency and consistency in life has been called a conduit. A practical guide to Christian life and conduct is the Proverbs of the New Testament, filled with moral precepts which states the ethics of Christianity. The book of Hebrews presents doctrine, James presents deeds. James says if you believe them, live it, and agrees that faith that does not produce works is dead. A double minded man is unsuitable. Like Hebrews it is addressed to Christian Jews. James covers the problem of testing 1:1-18. The reality of faith 1:10-2:26. The proper use of tongue 3:1-18, admonition against worldly mindedness 4:1-5:6, Exhortation 5:7-20. This is practical application of 'How' you have been scripturally informed to respond to your questions and your problems. How you respond to an issue, will determine how long you are going to stay with that issue. If you don't know or don't understand you have every right to ask. If you lack wisdom, the How to get it is there. What do we do with the word of God? First, you must understand the purpose and significance of the word, the what, the How and why of it. Consider its value. Does what you're thinking line up with God's words? Does it glorify God and bring honor to him? Who is doing the saying of what you're hearing? If right, then you go ahead to receive it. Hear what its talking. Examine and apply it if it's useful for you.

Selfishness is not the root of strife but Proverb agrees that it is Pride, which is the root of all strife, Proverbs 13:10. Motive is more valuable to God than gift or giving. Like Dr. Goodluck Jonathan, former President of Nigeria noted in one of his speeches, "the value of the process is more important than the product". As agreed by practicing

Christians, reason must go through the scripture to be reasonable. The truth you know is the truth that will set you free, it must go through the scriptures to be truthful, John 8:32. Dr. Mark Beliles and his colleagues in their book, Liberating the Nation wrote that, "we must reason from the totality of the Bible, not violating any principle while seemingly adhering to the truth based on a few scriptures" (McDowell and Beliles 1995, 99). A.W. Tozer in his book, the Pursuit of God, thoroughly analyzed the dangers of pride, calling it a burden that attacks the heart and mind and mentioning its brother and cousin, pretense and artificiality which should be avoided.

   1st Peter. Jesus lived the kind of life described in this letter, showing us that in this letter, that the secret of walking in newness of life or victorious Christian living is simply to acknowledge Jesus Christ and to rest on the blessed eternal fact of His sufficiency, 1st Peter 2:7. In Peter Chapter one, he tells us how to be pure and holy, 1st Peter 1:3-4, 22. This is done through love, James 2:5, Romans 13:8, and Mathew 22:37. Peter gives good plain advice on how we ought to live. The problem we have is in implementing what has been heard, leaving us again with the same question over what you do with what you've heard. We all know what Romans 10:17 has said, faith cometh by hearing and not by listening but hearing with your inner ears, which is your heart, and that's why He explained the how you ought to hear, in your heart, believe in your heart, unto righteousness and confession in made unto salvation. We required more emphasis on the How. This aspect reminds us of Robert E. Logan's comment in his book that some of books he had read and probably studied, "were full of helpful principles, but did not explain how to apply them" (Logan 1989, 11). This is one of the reasons why Christ has come to show us the 'How'. What 1st Peter is stressing, is the 'Hows' to do stuff. The sufficiency of God's grace and its practical application in relation to Christian living and endurance during trials and suffering should attract our attention all the time. When we ignore all these relational benefits, what shows up is Hebrews 2:3. We must live a balanced life involving Grace and faith. Grace provides, faith takes. Andrew Wommack did a good job in his book, The Balance of Grace and Faith, how you handle this issue will affect your lifestyle. Grace should balance Faith, Ephesians 2:8. Righteousness and justice should also balance each other, said by our Bishop Harry Jackson of Hope Christian Church, Beltsville MD.

What is Peter really saying in this 2nd epistle?

(1) He is talking about a living hope, which withstands the fiery trial.

(2) The conduct of the holy and royal priesthood. Chapters 2:9 – 4:19, and

(3) The service for the chief shepherd.

So basically, Peter is showing us How we are redeemed as in Hebrews 9:12, 15. The sinless life of Christ and his sinless blood sacrifice purchased both for us. And like quoted, "When once God's redemption comes to the point of obedience in a human soul, it always creates. If I obey Jesus Christ the Redemption of God will rush through me to other lives, because behind the deed of obedience is the reality of Almighty God" (Lebar 1995, 212). This redemption which involves regeneration, which is a change of nature from God, makes it possible for you to love your enemies, or pray for those who hurt you. Paul in Philippians 3:8 said that He willingly renounced all his earthly advantages and Jewish privileges as a means of attaining salvation. Remember that it's a process starting with Justification, which concerns a change of standing before God. Evangelist D.L. Moody enumerated the major points in that life altering transaction and wrote them on the Flyleaf of his Bible. (Branon 2010, 120).

Going through Justification, regeneration, repentance, conversion, adoption, sanctification, which is a change of service to God, meaning you have been sanctified and separated and finally Glorification. In chapter two, he is telling us how we can be able to live for Christ, 2:5-6, because we have been chosen to glorify Him 2:9.

What does it take for women to respect their husbands, and what does it take for the man to love his wife? Let us apply the principle of first mentioned and let's do first things first. See what the Bible says in Genesis 2:18. The man needs a helper and what it means here is that the man must provide the help that will make the woman a helper. The woman cannot give what she doesn't have. Train your child to drive, then he or she can become a driver. Give me something to hold then I become a holder. God has designed the man to head the family to love his wife, help her out, enable the woman, become a helpmate. Most people are operating with un-regenerated mind or expired mindsets and wonder why things are not working out as it should. Nothing just happens. As A.W. Tozer said in his book, "the purpose of God from the very beginning of creation is fulfilled in the regenerated heart of every believer who now can enjoy the manifest, conscious presence of the living God. The way into God's presence is the delight of the redeemed. It is where he belongs, naturally" (Tozer 2010, 121). The villagers who marry applies what the culture demands. Juniors to respect older people. Wives to respect their husbands. It is the tradition that mess up things. It is the tradition that contaminates the culture. How to carry out that culture is the problem. And that is why it is necessary, that we realize the scriptural 'Hows' that constitute foundation of theology. How do we apply the How to achieve your goal? How to use your suffering as a stepping stone to grow spiritually and that is why conduct is a requirement for the believer. Peter shows how Christ is the chief Shephard. We should all cast our cares on Him because He cares for us, 1st Peter

5:7-8, and in verse 8, the warning was given as in James 4:7 on how to handle issues concerning temptations of any kind. 1st Peter concludes with benediction.

2nd Peter. Warning was the main point that Peter expressed. Warning of danger with the church. It turned back to Hebrew 2:3.

Peter knew there was trouble and highlighted them.

(1) Peter knew that heresy often led to immoral living.

(2) Christianity must have a creed if right conduct is to be assured.

(3) Leaders were using the Church for money-making schemes.

(4) False teachers were laughing at the Lord's 2nd coming.

How can they avoid this? A full experiential knowledge of Christ is the stronghold against false teaching and an unholy life. 2nd Peter deals with things that pertain to life and godliness. In this issue, we should look at what was said. How do you adjust to accommodate what is said in 2nd Peter 2:3-4, and why it's said? He has given us all things pertaining to life and godliness. So, all the questions and answers have been dealt with. Warning against false teachers and How to avoid and recognize them have already been discussed. The return of the Lord and the day of the Lord were already explained. Peter has been aware of the confirmation of the prophecy of the OT. God's judgement upon men in ancient times, the flood and the overthrow of Sodom and Gomorrah. The closing exhortation is applicable to every child of God and can be accomplished only as the word of God is obeyed. They were assured of God's concern in reminding them of the things they have been taught and concluding in 2nd Peter 1:8 that if these things be in you and abound, they make you that ye shall neither be barren nor unfruitful in the knowledge of our Lord Jesus Christ. It is always reminding us not to forget to remember. Even when we do, the Holy spirit will put to our remembrance, pulling from our subconscious mind to our conscious mind.

1st John. The gospel of John sets forth the acts and words which prove that Jesus is the Christ, the son of God. It leads us across the father's threshold. The epistle makes us at home in the Father's house. It is an affectionate letter from our Father to His children in which He exhorts us to cultivate that practical goodness which brings perfect fellowship with Him. The gospel of John was written to give a foundation of full assurance of faith. Why all this? To let the believers, know that they have eternal life and to debunk the mistaken belief that knowledge was the means of salvation (rather than the cross). This was how Adam and Eve were deceived into thinking that it was through knowledge that man may be like the most High God. Andrew Murray in Education that is Christian by Lois E. Lebar, page 152, had already said it. His attraction was the fellowship (a) in the father's family covered by 1st John 1:1-4 and fellowship with God who is light 1:5-2:29 and (c) fellowship with God who is love, 4:7 – 5:12. John taught that obedience to God's commandments was a test of having the knowledge of God, John 15:9-17. Love makes you have a concern for the welfare of others. All sins are put into three categories. Lust of the eye, lust of the flesh and the pride of life. John's words imply that the complete conquest of all evil remains in us. There is a threefold earthly witness of faith, 1st John 5:6-8. Everything concerns the 'How' of the Bible.

2nd John. The second epistle of John is a letter to a member of that family, a lady Pastor. The letter was specifically to instruct the pastor as to her attitude towards false teachers. She was not to show hospitality to them. It was imperative that Christians denounce the false teaching in both word and attitude. It's important you know the truth, walk in the truth and uphold the truth against deceivers. Those who believe and maintain the truth of God must not compromise with error and must not do anything which would give aid and comfort to those who are spreading false teaching. This is how to avoid aiding and abetting evil.

3rd John. This short letter gives us a glimpse of certain conditions that existed in a local church in John's time. John commands and exhorts Gaius for his steadfastness and for his care of Christian missionaries, 3 John 3-8. And encouragement designed for Gaius until he John comes down to personally see him. He uses Diotrephes as an example of how not to live as a Christian, 9 – 11. He addressed Demetrius as having a good report of the truth, 12-14. The gospel of Christ rules out all teachings that are contrary to it, but unites all those who believe the gospel. Some of these illustrations are examples which we should imitate. Paul addressing the Philippian saints for their support Phil 4:19 and John here commending Gaius for his concerns 3 John 2. These are examples to imitate, even though some are using it as if it's God promising us, it's not very correct. It was Paul's wish for the Philippians (Philippians 4:19) as it was John's wish for Gaius (3 John 2); just putting you in remembrance of what has been said earlier.

Jude. "In the face of pressure to dilute pure Christian doctrine, Jude's readers are to stand firm and earnestly contend for the faith", verse 3. The presence of false teachers in the church and their activities in spreading their lying doctrines led Jude to write. He explained that the duty of Christians to keep themselves spotless and to contend earnestly for faith during apostasy should not be overemphasized. The first four verses covered his introduction and exhortation. Verses 5-7 deals with Historical examples of apostasy, verse 8-19, the description of false teachers and finally introduction and comfort, verse 20-25. The benediction closes the epistle of Jude.

Revelation. As the book of revelation revealed, it was designed to close the new testament revelation and to be the final inspired statement from God until the return of Christ himself. Rev 1:11, then turns to Jesus Christ signature tune, advising John to record or write down what you see, how you see it in other wards write down what I am saying, how I am saying and why I am saying it and make it available to the seven churches as directed. Like Ray.C. Stedman wrote in his book, Adventuring through the book of 1st Corinthians that "God designed us to learn, inquire and wonder, but never intended that all our knowledge should come from the world" (Stedman 1997, 28). He designed us to learn from Him, to seek our answers from Him and He provided the answers in the form of revelation in scripture and that's all my dissertation is explaining. So, our knowledge must have a right foundation he confirmed, by doing this, He is calling us back to the principle He laid down in the Old testament. This is the true source of knowledge and wisdom. That is where we begin, he remarked. The book of Revelation makes it clear that Christ and practicing Christians who thoroughly believe in the finished work of Jesus Christ are the ultimate winners in the game of life. I have discovered that the right knowledge and understanding of Revelation do motivate practicing Christians to consistent dedication and service. As alluded by writers, Rev 1:3 promises a blessing to those who read, understand, and obey the content of the book. On the other hand, Rev 22:18-19 promises a curse to anyone who add to or takes away from the book. These are right now being violated by some version of the bible writers or editors.

The promises made to those who overcome (Rev 2:7) appear to be promises to all true believers/practicing -Christians that will indeed inherit the promises of God per 1st John 5:5, and experience eternal life and fellowship with God. Ray.C. Stedman wrote that "God's word contains three thousand promises that are intended for our present, daily use" (Stedman 1997, 10). He asked How many have you claimed?

Every question has a scriptural promised answer and every problem has scriptural promised solution. The answer to that question will largely determine your effectiveness, your satisfaction and your happiness in the Christian life, so concluded Stedman in his opening comment of his series, 'Adventuring through Isaiah, Jeremiah & Lamentations' (Stedman 1997, 10). The scriptural promised answers and solutions could affect and change the way we pray. Psalms 91 and 103 do express the purpose of being in the right place at the right time, with the right attitude. The three books that are noted for prophecy are Ezekiel, Daniel and Revelation. The book of Revelation clarifies most of Daniels prophecy of the Old testament. As such understanding the prophecy of Daniel is of necessity.

While going through all these issues, Stephen McDowell and Mark Beliles, had this to say. "Every person has his outward and inward identity or individuality. Every person is responsible and accountable for his own choices and actions. For governments to be free, the people must assume this responsibility. Governments exist to secure those rights, like protecting the property of every sort, most importantly liberty of conscience. A free government will keep a balance of unity with diversity" (McDowell and Beliles 1995, 10-11). The question that goes out to us all is, why do we study the book of revelation, the purpose and significance of it all? The book of Revelation asks and answers are stated in its introductory note, written among other things from Nelson KJV study Bible.

(1) It was written to encourage believers to endure persecution knowing that there is light at the end of the tunnel.

(2) It shows the 'How' of it all, that the prophecy focuses on Jesus Christ, His person and His program for the world. So, knowing Jesus becomes all you need. His signature tune, that is the what, the How and the why of scriptures.

(3) The book attends to unite all the various lives of Biblical prophecy (both OT and NT) and to show how they converge upon the second coming of Christ to rule the earth in His Messianic Kingdom.

(4) The book seeks to correct some moral and doctrinal problems that exist (and still exist) in the churches and to instruct Christians in such things as salvation, prophecy, the person of Christ and Christian living.

(5) And finally, the book may be an attack on the paganism and emperor worship of the Roman Empire, particularly against the emperor Domitian and his persecution of Christians as at that time.

May be persecution of Christians seemed a logical way at that time for the Romans to overcome their troubles. Remember Tim Lahaye's comments on the purpose for the book of Rev, page 16. He touched on the promises of Rev 1:3. What the futures hold for you. Clearer detail concerning Bible prophecy than any other book in the Bible and finally that it's a book that completes the circle of Biblical truths. As Tim writes, it did clearly complete the great truths begun in Genesis and in other passages of the Bible. That is what the dissertation is saying that from Genesis to Revelation God has through the scriptures assured us of his two immutable things, the oat and the promise, in which it was impossible for God to lie, Hebrew 6:16-18. I will mention some of the illustration of Tim Lahaye in his book Revelation unveiled.

(1) "Genesis shows how human beings lost a chance to eat of the tree of life, Genesis 3:22-24. Revelation shows that human kind will yet eat of that tree, Rev 22:2" (Lahaye 1999, 16).

(2) Genesis tells of humanity's first rebellion against God, Genesis

3-4. Revelations promises an end to humanity's rebellion against God.

(3) Genesis shows the beginning of curse, Genesis 3:15-18. Revelation shows curse lifted, Revelation 22:3.

(4) Genesis promises that Satan's head will be bruised, Genesis 3:15. Revelation shows Satan bruised and defeated, Revelation 19:20.

The NLT study bible noted in its introductory remarks that the book of Revelation did appeal to the imagination and that readers will always benefit from picture-thinking. Revelation speaks through visions, images and figurative language rather than logical reasoning. Because of its nature, reading and understanding Revelation requires knowledge of imagination. We all observe that every man carries within himself or herself the history of the world and her people. Revelation seems to many a difficult book to understand especially when being read with a detached desire and willingness to comprehend. The questions, the problems and the doubts as to whether Christ's capability, availability and willingness be powerful enough to accomplish God's purpose of salvation, remains in the minds of the uninformed, Rev 6:9-10, the NLT. Introductory section answered that question in the affirmative, that despite all the evil in the world, however, revelation assured readers that the crucified and resurrected Lamb of God is truly the powerful Lion of the tribe of Judah (5:5-6). He is fully worthy to receive our praise, Revelation 5:11-13, NIV, as He is united with the eternal God. These angels declared that He was worthy to receive seven things; power, wealth, wisdom, strength, honor, glory and praise. They proclaimed his worthiness in Revelation 4:11 which fits being the anthem for people of Israel after crossing the Red Sea. Remember you are assured of protection and existence to safety. Fear not is used 365 times in the Bible assuring you of daily, 'fear not'. Jesus said, "I will never leave you nor forsake thee", Hebrew 13:5. We are assured that the best is yet to come. Billy Graham from his book 'Unto the Hills' said that the future is in the hands of one who is preparing something better than the eye hath seen or ear heard or has entered into the heart of man to conceive quoting from 1st Corinthians 2:9.

I will conclude this topic with the contribution attributed to Stephen McDowell and Mark Beliles in their book on Liberating Nations states briefly "that the principle approach to education inculcates in individuals the ability to reason from the bible to every aspect of life. We are supposed to, but do we? Do we really know how to reason from the bible to geography, astronomy, mathematics, or history not to mention national defense, foreign policy or civil government? The principle approach involves reasoning from the root or seed or principle to the facts of the issues. How do we solve the problems of varying views to issues? God has only one view to those situations, which we must understand if we desire to provide solutions for these difficult problems. Christians on both sides of the issue claim to have the bible as their base of belief, so why do they have opposite views? It is because they are not reasoning from the same biblical principle" (McDowell and Beliles 1995, 99). For me we are not reasoning from the intentions of the authors of these scriptures. The Bible advices us to enter into rest where the scriptural promised 'How' shows up.

C.S. Lewis in his book Mere Christianity raised a pertinent question and comment concerning Christian evangelism and when you look at what is happening today in the world no one will need a rocket scientist to tell you that things have fallen apart as Chinua Achebe rightly titled his book some years ago, 'Things Fall apart'. When you look at comments covered from pages 29 through 32 of Lewis' book, you will see how many times he used the word how. This is what my dissertation is addressing, the 'How' and 'Why' of the Bible. For sure

God has invested on us and needs a return on his investments. He created us on purpose for his purpose as Jeremiah 29:11 put it. For us to be able to get to that purpose we must address it from the why and how point of view which has remained an unanswered question, the How and Why issue.

What Lewis is seeking is this, "all I am doing is to ask people to face facts- to understand the questions which Christianity claims to answer" (Lewis 1980, 32). What he says makes a lot of sense. Like Dr. Vivian Jackson has said in her book, Where the Rubber Meets the road, "occasions of danger, risk, disappointment, and adversity, are where the rubber meets the road for all of us on planet earth" (Jackson 2003, 1). I completely agree with C.S. Lewis' view, because it's when we know better can we do better and when you see something can you say something. Remember you can't believe what you have no knowledge of. Your faith needs to be developed, Romans 10:17.

This is the time you start with the reasons why you must repent because of what happened in the Garden of Eden. The relationship we had with God was broken and sin really separated us from God.

There are facts and there are realities to deal with and the why and the how becomes the means of arriving at the answers to the issues raised by C.S. Lewis. There has been a rise of apologetic books in defense of the Gospel in the market.

"There are laws governing the universe. Evil is a parasite, not an original thing. The power which enables evil to carry on are powers given it by goodness. All the things which enable a bad man to be bad effectively bad are in themselves good things, resolution, cleverness, good looks. You can be good for the mere sake of goodness but you cannot be bad for the mere sake of badness" (Lewis 1980, 44-45). You can give without loving but you cannot love without giving. C.S.

Lewis did a good job here and NTS did a good job in choosing the books for this program. Lewis book, Mere Christianity, the triangular books of C.S. Lewis, Mere Christianity, Prof. Robert Lewis Wilkens, The Spirit of Early Christian Thought, and A.W. Tozer, the Pursuit of God, was a good trio to be referred to as and when due. Like C.S. Lewis said we must explain how we got into the present state of both hating goodness and loving it. If Adam and Eve had known the weight of the consequences, they could have thought twice in committing the crime of disobedience, that is eating from the tree of knowledge of good and evil.

Those two trees in the garden of Eden, were figuratively representing two solid foundations in Christianity, and have been a reference point in history, and as such bear the full mark of all generations. Lois E. Lebar's comment in his book, Education that is Christian, is self-explanatory. Let us see what Oswald Chambers said in his Studies in the Sermon on the Mount. "God's order was that the natural should be transformed into the spiritual by obedience; it was sin that made it necessary for the natural to be sacrificed, which is a very different thing. If you are going to be spiritual, you must barter the natural, sacrifice it?" (Chambers 1995, 36) Adam who heard all the instructions concerning the garden, and knew only how to obey God, silently and quietly bought into Eve's wrong idea that God may be hiding something from them regarding not eating from the tree of knowledge of good and evil. The Sabbath rest of the Bible started with Adam resting while God was bringing the animals for him to name them. This is the man who couldn't confront Satan's suggestion to the wife and so disobeyed God into eating with his wife from the tree of knowledge of good and evil. So, their natural eyes opened letting the Hell loose to the determinant of Adam and generations to follow. It was a perfect timing for Satan. For if Satan had waited, maybe they could have eaten from the tree of life and could have been too late for both parties. So, they were deceived into believing that they were to be better off and that the best could even get better, not realizing that the lust of the flesh, the lust of the eye, and the pride of life had taken them away from their daydream of being like God, as deceitfully suggested by Satan.

Now, that they had eaten from the tree of the knowledge of good and evil, good and evil must go together always. The law of opposites kicked in according to Tolle's book, the Power of Now, where you cannot have good without the bad (Tolle 1999, 24). This answers Lewis question of page 32 of his book Mere Christianity, because only God knew how we got there and only Him alone would be able to get us out. Mind whose instructions or suggestions you are considering outside the word of God. As a result of so much biblical ignorance afloat, we need to start from Genesis chapters two and three to give the whole concept of redemption as presented in the NT regarding the death, burial and resurrection of Jesus Christ, to the uniformed and unsaved and deceived people. Accurate biblical explanation and evangelism are necessary to enable people to understand the true purpose and significance of Christ atonement so as to be able to experience a genuine conversion. God did what only Him could do and through His only son redeemed those who would believe and receive the free gift of salvation and faith. To me evangelism should start with the why of the Bible for biblical understanding of the gospel and the How is used to bring in God's signature tune of What, How and Why. God used the Home, the family as the starting point, a place where His promises or the enemy's curses become a legacy. It all begins in our homes.

To me the summary of the Bible is about the study of the 'How' of all 'What' God said and did and 'How' of all the 'Why' God said and did. The 'All' is about God and the 'Every' is about us. Jesus confirmed this in Matthew 22:40, "on these two commandments hang all the law and the prophets". Also in Romans 12:3b, Jesus again assured everyone that believes the gift of salvation and faith; "According as God hath dealt to every man the measure of faith". The moral law per C.S. Lewis' book, Mere Christianity is all about what we ought to do. (Lewis 1980, 24). Remember the will of God as described in Romans 12:2, God's perfect will which is what you ought to do and God's acceptable or permissible will, which is what you like and want to do. Bear in mind what Deuteronomy 30:19 and Joshua 24:15 are saying, concerning your lifestyle in life, the choice is yours to make.

Review of Paul's stewardship shows how Saul/Paul was called by the resurrected Jesus to spearhead the spreading of Gospel of Christ to the Gentiles, Acts 9:1-18. I thought that Saul had a name change until I had Rabbi K.A. Schneider that Paul was his Roman name and Saul his Hebrew name. Paul was born in Tarshish by his Jewish parents who were Roman Citizens. Its observed that the apostles and other people of God were filled with the spirit and empowered to carry out the Great Commission of all people starting with the Jews, Romans 3:2. Acts highlights the ministries of Peter Chapter 1-12, Paul Chapters 13-28 which were committed to Paul, the oracle of God and shows that the Christian faith truly fulfills God's promises in the Hebrew scriptures chapter 2:16-36 to 4:11-12. Besides the apostles proclaiming that the death and resurrection of Jesus Christ was God's plan in fulfilling the Bible prophecies, did also show the importance of the individuals involved who God chose to carry his message and to testify about Christ. As Luke noted that except for Christ himself, Paul did more than any other person in shaping of Christianity. Through a life-changing, personal revelation of the resurrected Jesus chapter 9:3-6, 22:6-10; He did a lot for the ministry. Saul was radically and thoroughly converted through a process that transformed him and set the course on fire. Gary Inrig said in his book, Forgiveness, that "the line dividing good and evil cuts through the heart of every human being" (Inrig 2005, 26). Adam ate the tree of the knowledge of good and evil and since everyone existed in seed form within Adam, we all come down spiritually dead at birth, Romans 5:12. That is nothing but dead men walking and we still see a lot of dead people walking with their nature yet to be altered through regeneration. Most of the questions which people had been looking for answers have been scripturally addressed. Many of the problems both at home and abroad have been addressed and solutions offered. The difference between How we respond to issues before and after the cross have been highlighted.

Let us now focus on knowing what is of God, the 'How' that is of God and the 'Why' that is of God. Let us learn how to apply this in our lives. This implementation, when appropriately done, will open the door with spiritual illumination to our locating the scriptural precious promises of God regarding the answers to our questions and solutions to our problems. This simply reminds us of 2nd Peter 1:3, where God said that he had divinely given us all things that pertain unto life and Godliness.

God has endowed us with the intuitive knowledge of Him and the spiritual instinct within us from creation and as such we have no reason not to believe Romans 1:19-20. As A.W. Tozer said, "a Christian is one who has had the laws of God inscribed in his heart at the motivational center of his life. That is a Christian. Nothing else qualifies. With this new birth, this regeneration, comes an instinct that does not need exterior pressure to act" (Tozer 2010, 117). Professor Robert Louis Wilken dealt with reason which I had earlier referred to. He said that reason has to be loose or detached from religious faith for the mind to reach its full potential (Wilken 2003, 163). Remember what Eckhart Tolle said about identifying yourself with your mind. This has been dealt with earlier.

It is the purpose of this dissertation to bring to focus all what God has said and done, How He said it and did it, and why He said it and did it. This is to let you know and know there are scriptural promised answers to your questions and scriptural promised solutions to your problems. The key is in your hand and it's all about knowing Jesus, the author and finisher of your faith.

We can now see the power of 'How', and understand the significance of God's signature tune. It's about what is said and done. It's how it's said and done. It's why it was said and done both in the Old Testament time and now in the New Testament. In New Testament Jesus came down to confirm, pay the debt, reconnect and established the process for spreading the good news of His gospel. It's now what did Jesus say and do. It's all about How He said it and did it and why He said and did it. That Christ's signature tune, the New testament Anthem. Bill Crowder is about discovery series, mine will be about the 'How' series of the bible. Ray. C. Stedman, adventuring through the book of the Bible, mine will be Adventuring through the 'How's' of the Bible from Genesis to Revelation. The goal is to bring to focus, Eye-level perception, the How's of the Bible. God's signature tune. Again, thanks to the NTS team for the opportunity given me to undergo this TH.D program.

If you are not there yet, be sure you turn to believe and receive Christ as your personal savior. Remember what William Shakespeare wrote in Julius Caesar. The time is now, "that there is a tide in the affairs of men which, taken at the flood, leads on to fortune, omitted, all the voyage of their life is bound in shallows and in miseries. On such a full sea are we now afloat and we must take the current when it serves or lose our ventures" (Shakespeare 1982, 203-204). This is the appointed time, the set time. To be what you are supposed to be, you must remove what you were not created to be as your success depends on doing what you are created to do. It is time for believers to start believing and for partakers to start partaking.

Conclusion.

If those of us who are professionals, handymen, inclusive will make use of the Bible as believers, as we make use of our text books, our research findings, its applications with the professional skills and eagerness as required, we will all see how we will be transformed along with the society. God has wired us all differently, giving each of us something unique and specific to enable us to accomplish the purpose for which He created us. He has provided the 'How' to deal with all things pertaining unto life and godliness of 2nd Peter 1:3. The problem is always with the what and the why inherent in us, which of course is settled by the presence of the Holy Spirit for those who believe. He tells us the why of what God has said and done, the How Jesus has confirmed and established the principles governing all the How's of God. Again, in 1st Peter 5:5-8, Peter is vividly telling us the How, How God honors us individually and collectively if we can humble ourselves, since the grace of God will have no problem travelling if humility is available.

This is Trinity at work with the What, the How and the Why (W.H.W), which is God's signature tune. Proverbs 15:33 and 18:12 are living witnesses, regarding the role of humility as stated, "before honor is humility". God has put something into each hand and showed this in Exodus 4:2 by asking Moses what he has in his hand and as Elisha in 2nd Kings 4:2 asked the widow woman what she has in her house. Their faith was needed to meet their needs accordingly.

In Luke 8:43-48, the woman with the issue of blood made use of the power of now, per Eckhart Tolle's book, the Power of Now. She repositioned herself, and with courage, exposure and knowledge of the past and Power of now, went head-on to touch the border of Jesus' garment, for her healing. This woman said so, declared so, acted so and believed so, even when it wasn't so, for it to become so and with undiluted faith, the result she wished manifested. How? Because she spoke her wish into existence. God has said so; Jesus has confirmed so and the Holy Spirit a witness to the whosoever and whatsoever of the Bible. This collaborated with what Paul said in Philippians 3:13, concerning the power of now, in dealing with the present and forgetting the past.

Some of us are at the school, but we are not present. The lesson for us here is for us to stop looking down on what we have at hand, as nothing or not enough, knowing that when God is involved, the little becomes more, and even more than enough and the impossible becomes possible with the assurance of God's capability, availability and willingness. The problem is that many people who are Christians are not yet discipled.

Finally, the importance of God's scriptural signature tune cannot be overemphasized; the What, the How and the Why. We can sing it, dance it, hold seminars, revivals, crusades, workshops and conventions about it or can even pray and fast about it, but if we continue to neglect its application in our lives, it will end up like Bible saying of faith without works is dead. Remember and note the tunes of church songs, songs like, "thou art worthy Oh Lord" of Revelations 4:11 or 'Knowing you Jesus', the all in all song of Graham Kendrick, nor can we overlook the touchy song of Travis Greene; "You made a way, when our backs were against the wall. You made a way where there was no way. Don't know how, but you did it, you made a way. Now we are here, only because you made a way".

All these go to show God's concern over His created order, especially the human race. I agree with some people who have said and written that the Bible is a love letter to human beings for information and necessary action for those who will be willing and obedient to receive it, read, hear and accept the content of the letter and be able to trust and obey, as there is always a godly there for everybody, 1st Kings 17:4. It's the same system in the government circles for communications to bear that mark, for your information and necessary action. The Bible here also bears the mark of God's signature tune. This concludes my dissertation that the Bible bears the mark of God's capability, availability and willingness and promises that all questions of concern, all problems of concern have scriptural promised answers and scriptural promised solutions with the How you ought to and Why you must do it God's way. When done this way, we minimize the human "I" and human "me" and we even minimize the "me" generation issue with 1st Corinthians 4:7 in mind. The best reason for my recommending that you study and master God's Signature tune is that in this way you will discover better ways of harnessing God's promises, experiencing his love and thereby glorifying him and revealing his character to others. To demonstrate this desire of glorifying and bringing honor to God is like the rubber meeting the road as earlier stated by Dr. Vivian Jackson of Hope Christian Church in Maryland USA. Let's make the mastering of the contents of this book a vital and central topic to your ministry and for people involved in evangelism. Again, a special thanks to all the Directors, Management and Staff of Newburgh Theological Seminary Indiana.

References

1. Banks, James. 2014. *Let's Pray: Talking to God with the Words of the Bible.* Grand Rapids, MI: Discovery House Publishers.

2. Baxter, J. Sidlow. 1996. *Explore the Book: A Survey and Study of Each Book from Genesis through Revelation Complete in One Volume.* Grand Rapids, MI: Zondervan.

3. Bettensen, Henry and Chris Mauder. 1999. *Documents of the Christian Church.* 3rd Ed. New York, NY: Oxford University Press.

4. Bevere, John. 2011. *UnderCover: The Promise of Protection under His Authority.* Nashville, TN: W Publishing.

5. Branon, Dave. 2010. *A Story is Told: Inspiring Stories and Illustrations from Our Daily Bread.* Grand Rapids, MI: Discovery House Publishers.

6. Byrne, Rhonda. 2006. *The Secret.* New York, NY: Beyond Words Publishing.

7. Chambers, Oswald. 1992. *My Utmost for His Highest.* Edited by James Reimann. Grand Rapids, MI: Discovery House.

8. Chambers, Oswald. 1995. *Studies in the Sermon on the Mount: God's Character and the Believer's Conduct.* Grand Rapids, MI: Discovery House Publishers.

9. Collins, Gary. 2007. *Christian Counseling: A Comprehensive Guide.* 3rd Ed. Nashville, TN: Thomas Nelson.

10. Conner, Kevin. 1982. *The Foundations of Christian Doctrine: A Practical Guide to Christian Belief.* Portland, OR: City Christian Publishing.

11. Crowder, Bill. 1998. *Joseph. Overcoming Life's Challenges.* Grand Rapids, MI: RBC Ministries.

12. De Haan, M.R. 1978. *Broken Things: Why We Suffer.* Grand Rapids, MI: Discovery House Publishers.

13. De Haan II, M.R. 2007. *The Daniel Papers. Daniels Prophecy of 70 weeks.* Grand Rapids, MI: RBC Ministries

14. Erickson, Millard. 1998. *Christian Theology.* 2nd Ed. Grand Rapids, MI: Baker Academic.

15. Evans, Tony. 2014. *The Power of God's Names.* Eugene, OR: Harvest House

Publishers.

16. Evans, Tony. 2013. *Destiny: Let God Use You Like He Made You.* Eugene, OR: Harvest House Publishers.

17. Evans, Tony. 2011. *Victory in Spiritual Warfare: Outfitting Yourself for The Battle.* Eugene, OR: Harvest House Publishers.

18. Geisler, Norman L., and Ronald M. Brooks. 1990. *When Skeptics Ask: A Handbook on Christian Evidences.* Grand Rapids, MI: Baker Books.

19. Inrig, Gary. 2005. *Forgiveness: Discovery the Power and Reality of Authentic Christian Forgiveness.* Grand Rapids, MI: Discovery House Publishers.

20. Kunneman, Hank. 2016. *Prophesy with the Wind of God in Your Mouth.* Omaha, NE: One Voice Ministries.

21. Iverson, Dick and Bill Scheidler. 1976. *Present Day Truths.* Portland, OR: City Bible Publishing.

22. Jackson, V. Michele. 2003. *Where the Rubber Meets the Road: Surviving and Thriving in the Midst of Crisis.* USA: Zondervan Publishing House.

23. Keyes, Ken Jr. 1975. *Taming Your Mind.* Coos Bay, OR: Living Love Publications.

24. Kunneman, Hank. 2009. *The Revealer of Secrets: There is a God in Heaven Who Wants You to Know His Secrets – Learn to Hear Them.* Lake Mary, FL: Charisma House.

25. Lahaye, Tim. 1999. *Revelation Unveiled.* Grand Rapids, MI: Zondervan.

26. Lebar, Lois. 1995. *Education That Is Christian.* Colorado Springs, CO: Chariot Victor Publishing.

27. Lewis, C.S. 2011. *The Story of a Converted Mind.* Grand Rapids, MI: RBC Ministries.

28. Lewis, C.S. 1980. *Mere Christianity.* New York, NY: HarperCollins Publishers.

29. Logan, Robert. 1989. *Beyond Church Growth: Action Plans for Developing A Dynamic Church.* Grand Rapids, MI: Baker Book House Company.

30. McDowell, Stephen and Mark Beliles. 1995. *Liberating the Nations: Biblical Principles of Government, Education, Economics, & Politics.* Charlottesville, VA: Providence Foundation.

31. Meyer, Joyce. 1995. *Battlefield of the Mind: Winning the Battle in Your Mind.* New York, NY: Faith Words.

32. Murray, Andrew. 1888. *The Spirit of Christ.* London: Nisbet and Co.

33. Pearlman, Myer. 2007. *Knowing the Doctrines of the Bible.* Springfield, MO: Gospel Publishing House.

34. Perdue, Lawson. 2014. *The Power and Life of The Word.* Colorado Springs, CO: Charis Christian Center.

35. Reid, Garnett. 2014. *Old Testament Survey: Broadening Your Biblical Horizons, Part 2, Job - Malachi.* Wheaton, IL: Evangelical Training Association.

36. Roper, David. 2008. *Teach Us to Number Our Days.* Grand Rapids, Michigan: Discovery House.

37. Shakespeare, William. 1982. *Julius Caesar.* Edited by H.M. Hulme. Bungay, Suffolk: Longman Group Limited.

38. Shakespeare, William. 1977. *Macbeth.* Edited by Roma Gill. Oxford, Great Britain: Oxford University Press.

39. Stedman, Ray. 2016. *Why Doesn't God Answer Me: Trusting in Times of Doubt and Trial.* Grand Rapids, MI: Our Daily Bread Ministries.

40. Stedman, Ray. 2005. *The Way to Wholeness: Lessons from Leviticus.* Grand Rapids, MI: Discovery House Publishers.

41. Stedman, Ray. 1997. *Adventuring through Isaiah, Jeremiah and Lamentations.* Grand Rapids, MI: Zondervan Bible Publishers.

42. Stedman, Ray. 1997. *Adventuring Through Romans, 1 Corinthians, & 2 Corinthians.* Grand Rapids, MI: Zondervan Bible Publishers.

43. Stedman, Ray. 1997. *Adventuring through Psalms, Proverbs and Ecclesiastes.* Grand Rapids, MI: Zondervan Bible Publishers.

44. Stedman, Ray. 1997. *Talking with My Father: Jesus Teaches on Prayer.* Grand Rapids, MI: Discovery House Publishers.

45. Tidwell, Charles. 1985. *Church Administration: Effective Leadership for Ministry.* Nashville, TN: Broadman & Holman Publishers.

46. Tolle, Eckhart. 1999. *The Power of Now: A Guide to Spiritual Enlightenment.* Novato, CA: New World Library.

47. Tozer, A.W. 2016. *Alive in the Spirit: Experiencing the Presence and Power of God.* Compiled and edited by James Snyder. Minneapolis, MI: Bethany House Publishers.

48. Tozer, A.W. 2014. *The Pursuit of God*. Middletown, DE: Millennium Publications.

49. Tozer, A.W. 2010. *Experiencing the Presence of God: Teachings from the Book of Hebrews*. Edited by James Snyder. Minneapolis, MI: Bethany House Publishers.

50. Virkler, Henry and Karelynne Ayayo. 1981. *Hermeneutics: Principles and Processes of Biblical Interpretation*. 2nd Ed. Grand Rapids, MI: Baker Academic.

51. Wagner, Peter. 1996. *Spiritual Warfare Strategy: Confronting Spiritual Powers*. Shippensburg, PA: Destiny Image Publishers, Inc.

52. Warren, Rick. 2002. *The Purpose Driven Life: What on Earth Am I Here For?* Grand Rapids, MI: Zondervan.

53. Wilken, Robert. 2003. *The Spirit of Early Christian Thought*. New Haven: Yale University Press.

54. Womack, Andrew. 2007. *A Better Way to Pray: If Your Prayer Life Is Not Working, Consider Changing Directions*. Colorado Springs, CO: Harrison House Publishers.

55. Wommack, Andrew. 2009. *Balance of Grace and Faith*. Tulsa, OK: Harrison House.

56. Wommack, Andrew. 2009. *Living in the Balance of Grace and Faith: Combining Two Powerful Forces to Receive from God*. Tulsa, OK: Harrison House, LLC.

57. Wommack, Andrew. 2009. *The Believer's Authority: What You Didn't Learn in Church*. Colorado Springs, CO: Harrison House Publishers.

58. Wommack, Andrew. 2005. *Spirit, Soul & Body*. Colorado Springs, CO: Andrew Wommack Ministries, Inc.

59. Young, WM Paul. 2007. *The Shack*. Los Angeles, CA: Windblown Media.

CPSIA information can be obtained
at www.ICGtesting.com
Printed in the USA
BVOW10s1118261117
501238BV00002B/116/P